Dear Romance Reader,

Welcome to a world of breathtaking passion and never-ending romance.
Welcome to *Precious Gem Romances*.

It is our pleasure to present *Precious Gem Romances,* a wonderful new line of romance books by some of America's best-loved authors. Let these thrilling historical and contemporary romances sweep you away to far-off times and places in stories that will dazzle your senses and melt your heart.

Sparkling with joy, laughter, and love, each *Precious Gem Romance* glows with all the passion and excitement you expect from the very best in romance. Offered at a great affordable price, these books are an irresistible value—and an essential addition to your romance collection. Tender love stories you will want to read again and again, *Precious Gem Romances* are books you will treasure forever.

Look for fabulous new *Precious Gem Romances* each month—available only at Wal★Mart.

Kate Duffy
Editorial Director

PEOPLE WILL TALK

Carol Rose

Zebra Books
Kensington Publishing Corp.

http://www.zebrabooks.com

ZEBRA BOOKS are published by

Kensington Publishing Corp.
850 Third Avenue
New York, NY 10022

First Printing: June, 1999
10 9 8 7 6 5 4 3 2 1

Printed in the United States of America

For Randy Doss,
for his generosity of
time and technical knowledge
and his quiet, kind spirit.

Chapter One

If nothing else, the scandal surrounding Nora Elizabeth Hampton proved how unreliable men really
were. Total independence was her new motto. And
yet, here she was, waiting to ask Bret Maddock a huge
favor.

Bret stood in the temporary corral set up in the
corner of the pasture, his legs braced as he wrestled
a yearling calf off its feet. He wore no hat, and the
clear Texas sun glinted off his rumpled dark hair.

Shutting the truck's door behind her, Nora stepped
forward. With the noise and activity in the corral, her
presence went unnoticed for the moment.

She couldn't help watching Bret as she walked up
to the pen. He looked somehow different than she'd
remembered. In high school, he'd been everyone's
favorite bad boy, too good-looking to be missed and
too reckless for a girl like Nora.

They'd traveled in very different groups back then,
but even though she'd gone steady with Richard since

her sophomore year, she'd noticed Bret. What girl hadn't?

Now the wild boy had been transformed into muscle and sinew that shrieked sex appeal and danger all at once.

Bret held the calf down effortlessly, restraining its struggles as he threw a joke at the cowboy doctoring the animal.

Nora watched him, repressing a shiver in the unusually warm January air. Even as a kid, Bret Maddock had lived life by his own rules. Instinctively, she knew that hadn't changed.

For a woman who'd always done her best to play by the rules, Bret was a mine field of disruptiveness. He did what he wanted, never worrying that the next step could mean the end of someone's goodwill.

No one knew better than Nora how easily goodwill could be lost. Coming back to Stoneburg had taught her that.

One crazy moment had changed her life with Richard. Through no fault of her own, her engagement had ended. And here she was, home again after six years, waiting to make Bret a business proposition he didn't need and probably wouldn't want.

She'd already had one stable refuse to board Chessie. "No room," they'd said, but Nora suspected otherwise.

Just how fast did gossip travel? Had Bret heard about her disgrace? And if so, would the county's most notorious rule-breaker refuse her offer just because Nora had accidentally become Stoneburg's scarlet woman?

Resting her hand on the cool metal fence, Nora waited, unsure as to what his response would be. Since she'd come back to town, people she'd known off and on all her life had been staring at her as if she'd turned into Jezebel. Would Bret condemn her, too?

The calf that was pinned under Bret's knee bawled a protest. As the cowboy finished his task, Bret straightened, allowing the yearling to scramble up and trot off.

A cowhand said something to Bret, nodding in Nora's direction.

He turned and their gazes caught. Nora's heart increased its rhythm. A slow grin eased onto Bret's face, recognition immediate in his eyes.

He walked toward her, his long shotgun chaps molding the length of his muscular legs. Nora swallowed and focused on Bret's face. She'd been acquainted with Bret Maddock all her life, but she'd never had to come begging before, never needed him like she did now. Telling herself she'd find another answer if he refused, she watched him move toward her.

He walked with innate confidence with just the hint of a swagger, as if he'd never known himself to be unwelcome, or never cared if he were.

"Well, if it isn't Nora Hampton." He stripped off his leather gloves, his brown eyes alight with masculine interest.

"Hello, Bret." Nora said coolly. The very fact that she needed his help made her more prickly.

"You look good." His eyes narrowed as he flashed a glance over her, lingering for a second on the roundness of her breasts.

"Thank you." She fought down the sensation of tightness in her throat. Some things hadn't changed. He still looked at her as if he appreciated the scenery.

Bret leaned against the temporary fence panel, his tanned forearms bared by rolled-up sleeves.

Determined not to succumb to his masculine

charm, Nora forced a friendly smile. "It looks like you've been keeping yourself busy. Mother mentioned that you've taken on running the ranch since your father retired."

"Yep. Dad had no choice but me since his eldest son took up lawyering and moved to Dallas," Bret joked.

"Richard and I saw Ben at a party last year," she said without thinking, then stopped. Richard was the last thing she needed to talk about. "Ben seemed to be doing well," she finished quickly.

"Happy as a clam," Bret agreed, his eyes not leaving her face. "So what can I do for you, Nora Elizabeth? Assuming you didn't just stop by to watch us rolling in the dirt."

His words reminded her of her purpose, so Nora shoved her embarrassment aside. "I came to ask you a favor."

A smile curled at the corner of his mouth as his eyes darkened. "Just name it, honey."

Nora's heartbeat stumbled. Pressing on, she took a deep breath. "Hoyt Daniels down at the feedstore suggested I ask you about boarding Chessie. He said you'd kept his granddaughter's horse last year as a personal favor to him. I'd pay you, of course."

Nora met his gaze steadily, very aware that the Maddock Ranch didn't need the small amount she could pay.

"So you're planning on staying in town awhile?"

"Yes," she said firmly, her chin coming up. "I'm staying. And I'm starting an equestrian academy to teach English style riding and equitation."

Bret recognized the look on Nora's face. Determination gleamed there, reminiscent of the girl he'd known years ago. It seemed she had a dream, despite the scandal that had followed her from Dallas.

He shook his head, not bothering to hide his smile. "Honey, when you pick a goal, you do it with gusto."

"What do you mean?" she challenged.

"Just that this is Texas," he said with emphasis on the state's name. "It may not be where the west began, but its where the west is done best. And you want to teach *English* riding?"

"There's nothing wrong with variety," she defended. "Equitation is wonderful for teaching discipline."

He liked the fire in her face, the way she lost her cool when sparked. The Nora he'd known as a kid had always intrigued him with her curvaceous body and perfect grades. While he'd raised hell and majored in rodeo, she'd been student body vice president and queen of the honor society. A deliciously reserved girl with flashes of spirit in her eyes. Who'd have thought that her life would crash and burn?

With her brown hair glinting in the sunlight as it rippled to her shoulders, and her slender body filled out in all the right places, Bret could see why she'd attracted the wrong kind of attention. But he couldn't see her cheating on her fiancé.

Richard had been made for the business world, sucking up to the next big deal. If anyone would be unfaithful, it would be Richard.

"Will you let me board Chessie?" Nora asked again.

"Sure," said Bret, enjoying the relief that washed over her expression.

"I'd like to lease the use of a riding ring, too."

"I think that can be arranged," he agreed.

"About the cost," she said, raising her chin again. "I can't pay much, but—"

"Why don't you pay what Hoyt did?" said Bret, knowing he'd surprised her. He'd charged Hoyt two-thirds of the going rate. "We'll just call it a personal favor."

"Are you sure?" Nora said with a puzzled frown. "I could manage to pay—"

Bret interrupted her. "Why don't I ride back to the barn with you and show you where you can stable Chessie."

"Okay." A hint of wariness lingered in her eyes.

Repressing a smile, Bret turned back to the cow-hands still doctoring the calves. "Sam, you guys finish up here. I'm going back to the ranch with Miss Hampton."

Vaulting easily over the fence, he followed Nora to where the truck and horse trailer waited. "This is Hoyt's truck, isn't it?" he mentioned as he got in the passenger side.

"Yes," she admitted. "He loaned it to me to move Chessie."

Nora started the truck with a mixture of relief and suspicion. She wasn't sure she wanted Bret doing "personal favors" for her. Coming from him, it seemed too . . . personal.

On the drive over here, Hoyt's old truck had seemed as huge as a boat, but with Bret's long frame occupying the cab with her, Nora suddenly felt constricted in the space.

She kept both hands on the steering wheel, her gaze pinned to the road.

Bret stared at her, his gaze slipping down her body in a slow perusal she tried to ignore. Failing miserably, Nora kept her eyes fixed on the road and searched diligently for something to distract him.

"I understand Bunny got married last year," she said.

"Yep, little sister found herself a Louisiana boy," Bret drawled, his intent gaze not wavering.

"That's nice." Glancing away from the potent power of his charm, Nora gave up the conversation and concentrated on driving.

Minutes later, they pulled up in front of the barn. Eager to remove herself from his disturbing presence, Nora jumped off the truck immediately, hurrying back to the trailer.

Chessie stood placidly in the trailer, lipping at some hay in the feeder.

Balancing herself on the edge of the trailer with one foot, Nora leaned into the front to unhook the mare's halter from the feedbox. When she jumped down and went around to the back, she found Bret opening the gate and settling it on the ground.

"Thanks," she said. Once the ramp was down, Nora unhooked the hose-covered chain behind the horse's rear and patted the chestnut mare on the rump. Chessie backed out of the trailer.

A rush of affection flooded Nora as she grasped the horse's halter. She threw her arm around Chessie, burying her face in the animal's coarse mane. "It's all right, girl. I found a place."

Some of her darkest moments had been eased by escaping to the stables. Nora had never been able to sell the horse even though Richard complained about the time she spent riding.

"She's a beauty." Bret's voice brought Nora back to the present. "Have you had her long?"

Nora nodded, feeling foolish that he'd witnessed her spontaneous embrace. "My father gave her to me when I graduated from college two years ago."

"That must have been right before he died," Bret commented.

"Yes," she said tersely, refusing to acknowledge the wave of grief that always threatened her when she thought of her father.

"That makes her even more special then," Bret said, his face gentle as he ran a hand down Chessie's neck. "Bring her on into the barn and we'll find a clean stall."

After seeing Chessie settled, Nora paid Bret for a month's stabling. Relieved to have the horse settled, she nearly jumped when Bret reached out and captured her hand.

"Don't you think we ought to shake on it . . . or something," he murmured, a wicked grin playing at the corners of his mouth.

Her hand felt lost in his, surrounded and suddenly sensitive.

"Of course," Nora lifted her eyes to meet his, a bolt of sexual attraction shooting through her. "I really appreciate your stabling Chessie for me."

"No problem."

"Well," she said breathlessly as she withdrew her hand. "I guess I'd better get Hoyt's truck back to him."

Bret's broad-shouldered figure became a silhouette in her rearview mirror as Nora drove away. Turning on to the blacktopped road, she tore her thoughts away from his distracting presence.

When she left the house this morning, she'd promised to meet her mother for lunch. Now she'd have to hurry or she'd be late.

Nora dropped the truck and trailer off at the feed-store, retrieving her small Toyota to drive the short distance to Maxine's Cafe.

Maxine's tables had long served the small town of Stoneburg. Although the chain pancake house on the highway had drained off some of its business, Maxine's still functioned as an impromptu gathering spot for the town.

Parking the Toyota, Nora braced herself for her

mother's displeasure. There had been many lunches with Mother at Maxine's. With her mother's ill health and habit of worrying, this one boded to be as entertaining as a trip to the dentist.

Nora searched for her mother as she let the café's heavy glass door close behind her. From the white gold-flecked Formica to the constant noisy clatter, Maxine's never changed.

Spotting her mother, Nora wove her way through the crowded tables. She'd hardly made it halfway through the crowd when she realized her progress was being monitored.

At the large round table in the corner, every eye seemed glued to her. Nora looked straight ahead and tried to keep from gritting her teeth.

The censorious stares were difficult to ignore, though, particularly since they came from women she'd known most of her life: Mrs. Brady, the reverend's wife; Mrs. Callahan, the mother of a school friend; Miss Thurman, the town librarian; Cissy Burton, a girl Nora had gone to high school with; and of all people, Wilma Worthington, Richard's mother.

She even saw Mrs. Turner, mother of the mayor of Stoneburg, and owner of the Turner property, which would hopefully be the future home of Nora's riding academy.

Suddenly conscious of her plain cotton shirt and snug jeans, and how rumpled her hair probably looked, Nora couldn't help hurrying to get past that table. As she edged by the crowded space, not one woman offered a greeting.

The cold silence followed Nora like muddy footsteps.

If Nora had known of the dirty rumors she'd face, she wouldn't have been so eager to come home. Although they'd spent summers in the bigger city of

Wichita Falls due to her mother's uncertain health and social inclinations, Nora had always considered Stoneburg home.

So she'd returned to the little Texas town unawares, dismayed to discover that Richard's mother had heard a very different story about the New Year's Eve fiasco.

Once Nora had arrived in town, the woman's poisonous accusations seemed to spread like an onslaught of fire ants. This was her first visit to Maxine's since returning, and her reception left her feeling chilled.

Finally making it to her mother's table, Nora slipped into a chair, feeling frustrated by the situation.

"When I say twelve o'clock, I mean twelve o'clock, Nora." Her mother's southern accent softened her words.

"Sorry, Mother," Nora said automatically. She'd learned long ago not to react angrily when her mother was upset. Sharon Hampton had borne a lot in her life.

"I ordered the salad for you since you were late." Her mother gestured to the plate of greens and chicken salad.

"Thank you." Nora picked up her fork.

"I suppose you've been out talking to people about your ridiculous riding stable idea," her mother complained. "I wish you'd consider my reputation."

"You were the one who originally had me take riding lessons," Nora reminded, her voice mild.

"When you were twelve years old and needed help with your posture," Sharon said with gentle reproof. "I never intended you to own a stable and actually teach riding."

"I know, Mother." Nora took a bite of salad and

tried to ignore the hissing conversation from the table in the corner.

"Your father didn't pay for you to have an expensive education so you could end up mucking out stables."

Nora sipped her tea. "A Fine Arts degree doesn't go very far in today's job market."

"If you have to work, you could do something more feminine. Miss Thurman has advertised for a librarian's assistant."

Glancing involuntarily at the corner table, Nora repressed an ironic smile. "I don't think Miss Thurman would be interested in hiring me for the job."

"And whose fault is that?" her mother said in a lowered voice. "I don't mean to criticize, Nora, but you handled that situation with Richard as if you'd never been taught better."

The chicken salad tasted like sawdust, but Nora kept chewing. She fought the urge to ask her mother how her upbringing was supposed to prepare her to deal with a sixty-year-old man sliding his hand down the front of her dress during an upscale cocktail party.

There didn't seem to be any acceptable way to form the question, just as there was no acceptable way to announce to the town gossips that she didn't deliberately seduce Richard's boss.

"I'm just glad your father's not alive to suffer this humiliation," Sharon Hampton complained tearfully, ignoring her half-eaten salad.

Nora repressed the urge to utter an impatient retort. She knew life hadn't turned out the way her mother planned. Not only had her insurance agent husband died before retirement, leaving her nearly penniless, but Sharon also suffered from a variety of physical ailments that only added to her displeasure with life.

"It's not like I wanted all this happen, Mother," Nora pointed out as gently as she could.

Sharon Hampton didn't respond, wiping at the corner of her eye with the flutter of a pale pink handkerchief.

Regret tugged at Nora. Even as a child she'd hated adding to her mother's disappointments. Now, they only had each other. Part of the reason Nora had come home to Stoneburg was her mother's tearful refusal to sell the house she'd first lived in as a young married woman.

After all those summers spent chasing a gay social whirl in Wichita Falls, Stoneburg was apparently home to her, too. The house and Nora's meager trust fund enabled them to get by, but now her mother had to face the stigma of Nora's disgrace.

The situation was incredibly unfair. The voices at the ladies' table behind Nora seemed to grow louder. Reaching across the table, Nora covered her mother's fragile hand with her own.

"Everything will be all right. With nothing else to feed it, the talk will die down eventually."

"I certainly hope so, Nora," her mother replied, her voice trembling. "For both our sakes."

Drawing her hand slowly from Nora's clasp, she picked up her small handbag. "I have a hairdresser's appointment, honey. You stay and finish your lunch."

Nora sadly watched her mother preparing to leave. She knew that Sharon's moments of anger stemmed more from embarrassment than from a lack of concern for her daughter.

"If you really want to redeem yourself," Sharon said, lowering her voice again, "you'll find yourself a respectable husband as quickly as possible."

"I don't think that's the answer," Nora said steadily.

"Well, I guess you know best." Sharon picked up her cardigan and left the café.

Nora stared numbly at her chicken salad, swamped by a sudden urge to do someone bodily harm, preferably Richard, and then his boss. The old lech hadn't even had the excuse of being drunk when he pinned her against the counter in Richard's North Dallas home and proceeded to investigate the contents of her bra.

Still, violence wouldn't do her any good now. The engagement to Richard was over and strangely enough, as the shock was wearing off, Nora found herself relieved. They'd gone together most of high school. Over the years, she'd become accustomed to his presence in her life, never questioning whether that was what she really wanted. Now Richard had taken the matter out of her hands, and she found she didn't really miss him.

It was a joy to be back home in Stoneburg. At least, it was if she didn't glance around at the table behind her.

Hopefully, the town gossips were only a small portion of the population of Stoneburg. She'd just have to win over the rest of the people—the ones who'd grown up steeped in Western tradition, fiercely loyal to their style of horsemanship.

"Well, if it isn't my favorite riding teacher."

Nora jumped, startled by Bret Maddock's voice.

"You don't mind if I join you?" he asked, as he seated himself across the table in the seat Sharon had just abandoned.

"No, no, of course not."

A murmur rose from the table in the corner. Nora resisted the urge to look around, knowing that Bret's arrival and his choice of seats had not gone unnoticed.

Tossing his hat on a chair, Bret smiled at her. He carried a lot of voltage in that smile. Nora took a deep breath, trying not to absorb its impact.

"I'm starved," he announced. "Why don't you pour out your deepest secrets to distract me while I wait for my burger."

Nora frowned. Her deepest secrets? What was he up to?

"Okay," he conceded easily when she didn't speak, "if it's too soon for secrets, how about telling me all about your riding stable plans."

She tried to resist his lure, but he looked so endearingly confident, sitting across from her, so dangerously charming with his arms braced on the tabletop and his eyes fixed on her face with complete attention.

"Has anyone ever told you you're a little too confident?" she asked ruefully.

"All the time." He smiled again. "Is that gonna be a problem?"

The noise in the café seemed suddenly distant, the hum receding to leave them alone across the table. There was an intentness in Bret's face, a look in his eyes that she'd never seen directed at her before.

Please, Lord. Don't let Bret Maddock set his sights on me. With his reckless charm and potent virility, he was the last man she needed at this point.

Some women could grab hold of a comet and enjoy the ride, but Nora wasn't one of them. Bruised from her run-in with one man's selfish dishonesty, she didn't plan on exposing herself to Bret's brand of unreliability.

"What's the matter, Nora Elizabeth? Afraid I'm going to set myself up in competition? Maybe I'll start riding in those high boots and sissy pants."

Nora laughed, his teasing comment breaking some

of the tension. "I don't think there's much possibility of that."

"Probably not," he agreed.

She just couldn't see Bret doing anything as disciplined as riding English style. He'd been a hell-raiser since grade school.

"Equitation isn't risky enough for you," Nora said dryly.

"Why, whatever do you mean?" Bret leaned forward, elbows propped on the table, his face alive with teasing challenge.

"Nothing," she back-pedaled. "Nothing at all."

"Now, Nora," he chided. "Come clean."

"Well, you've been champion of the Montague Riding Club annual race ten years in a row," she said, grabbing at the first thing that entered her mind. "Rodeoing, bungee jumping, stunt flying. From what I've heard you do pretty much anything that involves risk to life and limb."

Bret smiled. "Now we're not going to listen to gossip about each other, are we?"

His question stopped her heart for a moment. Nora studied his face, unable to discern where he stood on the matter of her scarlet reputation. He'd clearly heard about the scandal.

"I hope not," she replied carefully. She didn't plan on signing up for his merry-go-round of feminine companionship, but she didn't plan to make an enemy of him, either.

"We'll make a friendly pact," Bret offered, raising his voice ever so slightly. "We'll tell each other our worst sins before the gossips do."

He glanced at the table of women behind her and back to Nora, winking. She couldn't help but laugh, although his antics left a queasy feeling in her stomach. It was like waving a red flag at an already irritated bull.

"I'm sure my sins aren't that interesting," she said quietly, "but the friendly part sounds good."

Other than Hoyt and Janie, Bret was the only person in town who treated her anything like a friend. The women whose eyes seemed to be boring into her back certainly didn't.

"I look forward to being friendly with you," he teased, "but let's don't forget to get back to the sins sometime soon."

Maxine approached with Bret's plate. "Here's your order, you rascal," she declared in a rough voice, worn by years of smoking. "Don't forget to pay for it."

"Since when do I forget anything?" Bret called after her.

The older woman laughed and kept on walking.

"So tell me more about the riding school," Bret said again before taking a bite of his burger.

Nora shrugged. "I want to teach riding to youngsters. Right now, I'm trying to start a business and get a bank loan."

Bret nodded. "Sounds like a good plan. But I think it'll be uphill work to get folks here excited about English style riding."

"Not young girls," Nora said positively. "Pre-teen and early teen girls take to equitation like ducks to water. It helps teach them responsibility for their mount and themselves. I promise, once I get going, I'll never have to groom Chessie again—I'll have kids clamoring to do it."

He looked skeptical. "Most kids around here have horses. They're not like city kids who have never cleaned out stables."

Nora shook her head. "Equitation is different. It

focuses on the relationship between rider and horse. Eventually, I'd like to have a stable and ring and a place to board horses."

"You ought to be able to find several good pieces of property to build on," Bret said, digging into his french fries.

"I won't be able to borrow enough to build," Nora said. "What I want is to find a place with the basic structures—stables for the horses and a working ring—already on it. Something I can fix up as I go along. I have a place in mind, but I'm not sure I can get a loan yet."

"You have a particular property in mind?" Bret asked before polishing off the last of his burger.

"Yes." Nora said, trying to keep a grip on her excitement. She'd been thrilled to find the perfect spot to begin her new life. "It's been empty for ten years now, but the barn is still sound and there's even a small farmhouse I could live in. It's the Turner acreage that runs along your western boundary."

Bret's hand paused in mid french fry lift. Surely, he hadn't heard her right. Nora wanted the Turner farm? Here was a potential complication in his carnal pursuit of her.

She hesitated a moment. "Mother really doesn't have room for me. But I'm staying with her until I can find a place."

Bret could understand why Nora was eager to have her own place. Still, given his own plans for that piece of land, her news about the property wasn't good.

"Have you given that place a good look-over?" he said casually. "It's been empty more like fifteen years."

"I know," Nora assured him, "but the buildings seem sound."

"Be a good idea to have someone in construction

check the place out before you get too far down the line.'' He swiped a carrot stick off her plate, deciding not to worry about something that might never come to pass.

''I will,'' promised Nora, stabbing a bite of salad. ''Hoyt Daniels says Mrs. Turner has a CPA that handles her business—a man named Jim Carlyle. I can't really approach him about the property until I have some paying students, but I'm determined to buy that land and set up my own stable as soon as possible.''

''Sounds like a plan,'' Bret said. She certainly looked determined, but the woman had a long road ahead of her.

A companionable silence fell between them as they ate.

''Can you believe her gall?'' The brittle, high-pitched voice floated from the table in the corner.

Cissy Burton went on, ''She sits right here among respectable people, just like she hadn't tried to ruin a man's life.''

Nora's hand clenched the paper napkin, her fork settling on to the salad plate with a faint clatter.

''Some women are born tramps,'' another woman spoke.

''She ought to be run out of town before she gets some other poor boy in trouble.''

Bret recognized the last voice as Wilma Worthington's. Naturally, she'd never think her perfect son had done anything wrong, so Nora must be to blame.

Glancing back at the woman across the table, Bret saw her transformed. Nora sat with a closed expression on her face. Only the firm line of her mouth gave a hint of her distress at hearing women she'd known all her life turn against her.

''Well, I wouldn't think she was pretty enough to

cause this much trouble," Cissy declared in a clear voice.

Bret heard Nora's swiftly indrawn breath. Something about the way she sat there silently drew his compassion—and made him fighting mad.

He leaned forward. "Cissy Burton needs a swift kick in the fanny . . . or a poke in the eye. Why don't you go over there and show her how it feels to be ground into the dirt?"

Nora looked up suddenly, her eyes dark with suppressed anger. "Reacting to people like that just gives them more ammunition. Eventually, it'll die down."

She glanced at her watch and grabbed for her purse. "I have to go now, I'm late."

He watched her exit with a bad taste in his mouth. Between the scandal about Richard's boss and Cissy's witchy attitude, Nora needed a friend. Bret figured he was well qualified, having survived a few scandals in his time. And if his bonus was getting a lot closer to Nora, well, sometimes life was good.

Chapter Two

Bret slung his saddle over the fence rail and tried not to look as if he were staring at Nora.

The mid-morning sun gleamed off Chessie's coat with a rich, polished glow. Nora moved around the riding ring as if she were part of the chestnut mare.

Smiling and sweet-talking her mare, she'd put the animal through its paces, riding around the ring in the peculiar bouncy English style.

He'd thought she'd looked good in jeans, but Nora in skin-tight riding breeches was a sight to behold. His mouth had gone dry when she walked past. Bret had never thought he'd get so turned on by a woman that fully clothed.

He dipped a rag in the can of neat's-foot oil and made himself concentrate on the saddle he was oiling.

Out of the corner of his eye, he could see the dark helmet perched on her red-brown hair, leaving only the twitchy end of a braid visible. She trotted the horse around the riding ring in a steady, precise manner, her voice low as she talked to the mare.

Something about her movements kept Bret staring.

Nora held herself poised in the saddle, using her legs as well as her hands to guide Chessie around the ring.

Bret watched her effortless communication with the horse, the tautness of her thighs and her straight posture that never seemed stiff. He couldn't help being impressed.

A change came over Nora when she was on horseback—she seemed supremely confident and comfortable. Every step, every turn was accomplished with a minimum of fuss, as if getting a nine-hundred-pound horse to do exactly what she wanted was as effortless as walking.

The slam of a car door drew Bret's attention away from the woman in the corral. A flurry of small footsteps echoed in the barn before Jessica McGarver shot through the open door and cast herself exultantly against the fence next to Bret.

"Gosh, isn't Chessie the greatest!" The ten-year-old girl looked at the mare in blatant adoration. "Nora's gonna let me ride her today!"

"Why don't you get excited about it?" Bret said dryly.

"Jessica, you left your coat in the car." A slender blond woman stepped out of the barn.

"Oh, Mom." The girl made a face. "It's warm."

"Put it on." Eve McGarver held out a jacket and waited until the child slipped it on.

"Anyone would think you never let this kid out of the house, the way she's so revved up about these lessons," Bret commented.

Eve sighed. "She's always revved up, Bret, but not usually this bad. She'll probably be a total zero in school tomorrow."

Bret smiled. Eve taught elementary school and

everything about her looked the part. Her short hair was both stylish and practical and, from what he could tell, her wardrobe consisted of craft-decorated tops and skirts.

"Jessica's teacher is at her wits' end," Eve murmured.

With her thin, leggy body draped against the fence, Jessica was so engrossed in watching the horse she didn't seem to hear them.

Bret and Eve both watched the activity in the riding ring.

"Nora's wonderful on horseback," said Eve, her face softening as she watched her friend.

"Amazing," Bret murmured, still captured by her skill.

"I've invited her to my classroom to talk about riding. I think the children will be very interested."

"Bound to be," he said. "Particularly if they get to skip an arithmetic lesson or something."

"Oh, you." Eve punched his arm playfully before returning her attention to the ring.

"Ouch." He made a show of rubbing his arm, but he'd lost Eve's attention.

"Nora gets on one of those huge animals and it's like she forgets everything else." Eve's eyes rested on her daughter before sending a meaningful glance Bret's way. "And there's so much to forget lately."

"Richard's an as—" he broke off when Eve frowned and looked quickly at her enraptured daughter. "He's an idiot," Bret amended.

"What I'd like," Eve said in a lowered tone, "is to give the old biddies in this town permanent detention for how they're treating her."

"What I'd like," Bret said, chuckling, "is to see Cissy Burton's face when you call her an old biddy."

* * *

An hour later, after Eve had taken Jessica home, Nora felt ready to fly. She'd taught her first lesson and knew she was making the right decision.

Jessica was a joy to teach. Nora was sure there were other girls in town who would want lessons, too.

The only flaw in the morning had been Nora's absurd awareness of Bret's presence. Why on earth couldn't he have been out wrestling cattle? Preferably out of her sight.

Nora took care of feeding and watering Chessie, giving her a final pat as she left the stall. "You did good today, girl. Pretty soon we'll be working every day."

The day had warmed up, but the barn held a lingering shadowed coolness. Nora took her jacket from the nail where it hung and made her way into the sunlight.

Bret stood by his pickup, loading various things into the bed. "Jessica seemed to be enjoying her lesson," he commented.

"Yes, she has natural ability," Nora agreed.

Compelled to escape Bret's heady influence, she edged forward. The man always managed to disable her brain while sending her heart racing. She didn't need the distraction. If even a straight arrow like Richard could betray her, how much more likely was Bret to do so? Bret had "fun" tattooed on his forehead. As sexy and disturbing as he was, she'd be an idiot to think he'd treat her heart any better than Richard had.

"Well, see you later," she said, turning toward her car.

"Hey," Bret called to her. "Do you have a few minutes to help me with something?"

Startled, she turned back. "I guess so. What do you need?"

He threw a pair of work gloves into the truck cab. "I have a small windmill repair to do and all the ranch hands are busy doing other stuff."

"Windmill repair? I don't know anything—"

"Don't need to know anything. I just need another pair of hands. It won't take more than an hour." Bret smiled as if he knew the turmoil in her head.

There wasn't really a way she could refuse him. She obviously didn't have a lot to do until her lessons picked up, and she felt as if she owed him something for agreeing to board Chessie at a cut rate.

"Sure. I guess I have some time." Nora steeled herself against his smile as she threw her jacket in her car.

"Good." Bret grinned as he got into the truck.

Nora climbed gingerly into the ranch vehicle after he swept several tools, a paper bag and a quantity of dust off the seat.

They drove away from the ranch buildings, taking a rough track into open pasture. Bret pointed out several landmarks, indicating the property line between his ranch and the Turner property. She scrutinized the land she hoped to buy.

How would Mrs. Turner respond to her offer for the land? Nora had known her for years and still couldn't guess where she stood. Sara Turner was a pleasant woman, the epitome of politeness. Even if she were scandalized by Nora's supposed indiscretions, she'd never be ill-bred enough to show it.

As they drove over the rolling January-brown hills, the battered pickup surprised flurries of crows from the occasional clumps of brush. The sun streamed down from a pale sky.

Nora drew in a breath of the warm air that blew

in through the crack of the lowered window. Despite the rumors, she'd done the right thing in coming home.

She couldn't help the contentment that seeped into her as she rode beside Bret in the bouncing pickup. Being with him might be dangerous to her peace of mind, but at least he didn't treat her like a scarlet woman.

The windmill was visible from down the hill, its old-fashioned blades a serrated circle in the sky.

Bret halted the truck at the base of the tower, a structure of galvanized iron that lifted the windmill head nearly fifteen feet off the ground.

It wasn't until they'd stopped and Bret had gone around to the back of the truck that Nora first thought to wonder what exactly Bret wanted her to do.

Getting out of the pickup, she waited as he carried several new windmill blades around and propped them against the tower.

"I tell you what," he said. "You climb up and I'll hoist the blades up to you."

"You want me to climb the tower?" Above them, the windmill whirred, its hum seeming part of the breeze that streamed past.

"Yeah." He gathered up tools and shoved them in his back pockets. "Just go up and reach down. The blades aren't heavy."

Thank the Lord she'd never been afraid of heights.

Bret looked up. "Just climb right up," he encouraged. "It's as safe as the back of a horse."

"Of course," she said as she placed her foot on the first rung. The metal felt warm to her hands. Once in motion, Nora refused to let herself stop. A brisk breeze darted playfully around the tower's legs, brushing at the wisps of hair that had escaped her braid. She kept climbing, her eyes focused on the rungs in front of her until at last she reached the top.

Clambering onto the small wooden platform, she glanced up to the full spread of sky and land.

"Okay," Bret called. "Turn around and lie on your belly. I'll hoist the blades up to you one at a time."

The platform was about five feet square. Abandoning any hope of gracefulness, Nora positioned herself on her stomach and reached down for the blade Bret offered. One by one, he raised up each curved metal piece until all three rested on the platform.

"Good. You stay there. I'll be right up." Bret turned to grab a pair of pliers off the bed of the truck.

Nora looked around the platform. He wanted her to stay up here while he worked on the thing? Good grief, there was hardly room for her and the blades, much less a broad-shouldered Bret.

The tower reverberated with Bret's steps on the ladder. Nora scooted to one side, trying to make herself small.

He poked his head through the opening, a wide grin breaking on his face. "Hi, there. Enjoying the view?"

She glanced out over the pasture, her senses still captured by his smile. "Yes, it's wonderful."

He climbed up and settled himself next to her, so close she could feel the warmth of his body and breathe deeply of his male scent.

Nora shifted closer to the edge.

"Here, hold this."

She took the tool he held out.

"One thing about windmills," he said. "They're simple machinery. We'll have these blades on in no time."

"Good." For heaven's sake, she scolded herself, how much less intimate could the situation be? She was perched on top of a windmill with the guy. People for miles around could see them.

But it didn't feel that way. With the wind sweeping silently around them, the world could have been an empty place.

Despite focusing her attention on anything but Bret, Nora was aware of his every movement. He handled the windmill as if it were a Tinkertoy, his work seemingly automatic.

Grasping the metal upright with one hand, Nora scooted to the edge of the platform to make more room for him.

"Hand me those pliers."

Surrendering the tool, she eased further away and risked dangling her legs off the platform.

All around her lay the glorious tapestry of prairie and sky. The winter grass rippled golden in the sun, hugging the ground. Each hill ended in a trickle of a valley where scrubby live oaks clustered.

Occasionally, crows lifted from the fields below, circling in a flurry of blue-black wings, only to settle down again near where they'd started as if involved in a shimmering, shifting dance.

The clunk of a tool against the platform behind her seemed like a minor accompaniment to the performance of the moment. Nora drew in a breath and held it like a treasure before allowing a sighing release.

"It's beautiful, isn't it?"

Bret's voice came from so close behind her that she jumped.

"Hey," he laughed, steadying her with his hands on her upper arms. "No swan dives allowed."

"No," she murmured shakily, acutely conscious of the heat and strength of his hands through the thin cotton of her shirt.

"This is why I do windmill work," he said. "On days like this the place looks like God's country from horizon to horizon."

Instead of letting go of her, he moved closer, sliding his arms around to hook together in front of her body.

Nora's heart started its own rendition of the "Star-Spangled Banner." Locked against him, she was surrounded by sensation, the warmth of him, the solid feel of his muscled chest.

"What I really love," Bret went on, "is the way the earth looks from the sky. Leaving the ground is so freeing."

His breath wafted against her ear, sending her nerve endings into a frenzy. She tried to hide the involuntary shiver that skated over her skin.

"I—I guess that's what you like about flying," she said, compelled to speak even though her voice felt strangled.

"Mmmhm." Bret leaned back slightly, settling her more comfortably against his chest. "I've always loved heights. Sometimes when I'm at the top of a tall building, I get the craziest urge to jump."

"That *is* crazy." She'd always known he had his moments of insanity, which made her intense attraction to him even more strange.

"Yeah," Bret said. "I guess the craziness explains my parachuting and bungee jumping phases."

Nora chuckled, tilting her head back to look at him. "Your mother must worry about you all the time."

His smile flashed and died as he looked down at her. She saw the darkening of his eyes, felt the tension in the moment, and knew that if she held still, he'd kiss her.

Yearning possessed her with an urgency. She knew

she couldn't trust him with her heart, that he was trouble, but now she just wanted to kiss him. The realization should have terrified her out of his arms and off the windmill platform.

But at the moment, she couldn't move. Nora's eyes fluttered shut as Bret bent closer. She felt the brush of his lips against hers, the soft catch of electricity that funneled through her body. He murmured something in his throat, pulling her tighter as he angled to taste her mouth.

The scent of him flooded her and left her hungry and aching. She opened to his kiss, welcoming the taste of him, the sensation of being surrounded by him. He kissed her with a softness that held no hesitancy, a thoroughness that sent a ringing to her ears and a rush of blood thundering through her body.

Never had she experienced such an overwhelming kiss.

She told herself to be grateful when he lifted his mouth from hers. It took all her effort to focus on that thought.

"I'm glad you came home, Nora."

Her eyes popped open.

"Now I know who to call when I need to do windmill repair."

She stared at him, dumbfounded by the chaos of her nervous system while struggling to return to the normal world of speech. Good Lord, she was acting as if she'd never been kissed before.

"Glad to be of help," she said as coolly as she could.

He laughed, keeping one hand on her arm as he shifted back to the center of the platform. She scooted after him, swamped with a sudden need to feel the ground beneath her feet.

Bret Maddock was the kind of guy who could make

a girl forget her upbringing and cast her reputation to the winds—and then go merrily on his way.

Following him down the ladder, Nora reminded herself of her situation. Because of Richard's betrayal, the town censured her for something she hadn't done. Trusting Bret was absolutely out of the question.

Hoyt's feed store always smelled the same. The odors of hay and pesticide mingled with the dusty scent of dog. Nora stood inside the door, her eyes adjusting to the sparse light filtering down from the occasional light fixture.

The dusty shelves were still crammed with feed and fertilizer. Along one wall hung all manner of harnesses and cinch straps. Even the old, bone-idle bird dog that was laying by the electric heater looked the same as the last time Nora had been here.

No matter how old she got, she'd always remember the combination of scents in this place. Hovering in the front of the door as memories flashed through her mind, Nora slowly became aware that she was the center of attention.

Although Hoyt was busy behind the counter writing out an order for a customer, the cluster of men sitting around the heater all stared at her.

Small towns were notorious for fostering interest in one's neighbors, but the expression on the faces watching her held more than friendly interest. There was an assessing quality to their stares, an overly bold, lingering inspection.

She saw their exchanged glances, their sly smiles, and she felt her backbone stiffen. Even here in this bastion of masculine activity, gossip reared its ugly head.

One younger man in particular looked her over, a smirk on his face as he pushed back his black cowboy hat.

A surge of frustration rose in Nora, and she squared her shoulders. She'd never realized how petty and small-minded people could be, and how quick to judge.

Moving forward with determination, Nora skirted the stacks of seed on the floor. She shuffled the flyers in her hands as she reached the bulletin board, turning her back on the group by the heater. Her purpose in being here had nothing to do with them, and if they chose to be rude, let them.

Irritated, she forcefully skewered her announcement with a push pin. Getting the riding academy going was the important thing.

She stepped back to make sure the paper was straight.

The announcement had turned out well. Even the gold-apricot paper was a good choice. "Announcing the Opening of the Stoneburg Equestrian Center," it said.

Smoothing the paper, Nora allowed herself a moment of pride. This business was her dream, and if she had to ignore several hundred rude people to get it going, she would.

Just then the door to the feed store swept open and crashed shut. Nora glanced up as footsteps echoed on the wood floor.

Wearing tight pink jeans and a fringed western shirt, Cissy Burton crossed the store, sashaying over to the heater with a flirtatious smile on her face. She placed her hand on the shoulder of the cowboy in the black hat, her voice pitched low and sultry as she leaned over to make some remark.

The men in the group grinned.

Nora looked away, remembering the girl she'd known in school. Even then, Cissy had worn tight jeans and lots of makeup, and would chase any guy that caught her eye.

Even though Cissy had been popular for obvious reasons, Nora had never envied her. Her flirtations always seemed desperate, her attention shifting quickly from one boy to another.

Cissy had boasted of her sexual conquests in a way that was distasteful to Nora. It always seemed as if Cissy was hungry to belong, always offering what she thought people wanted.

Her current animosity toward Nora probably stemmed from Cissy's high school crush on Richard. Before Nora started dating him, Cissy hadn't appeared to give her a thought, but since that time, the girl hated her.

Giving her announcement one more glance, Nora turned away from the bulletin board.

The black-hatted cowboy caught her gaze and held it before letting his stare slide down to her chest.

Nora felt the burn of his inspection from across the room; it was as if he believed that she was available to every man she met.

Lifting her chin, she met his stare angrily, resentment flooding her at this undeserved insolence.

The cowboy turned his head a little, still staring at her body, and made a comment to Cissy.

The group around the heater erupted in laughter, Cissy's high-pitched squeal rising above the men's chuckles.

Nora felt an angry knot of tension in her chest. For whatever reason, she'd become Richard's scapegoat, and the object of this idiot's moronic humor.

She grappled with the range of possibilities presented by her furious brain. Unfortunately, getting an Uzi and wiping them all out might lead to some jail time. They probably weren't worth it.

As Nora stood there, talking herself out of committing murder, a sneer appeared on Cissy's face. Challenge in her eyes, she pitched her voice louder and said, "I just hope Bret knows what he's doing letting slime like her crawl into his bed."

"Who says they do it in a bed?" the cowboy questioned with an ugly grin. "Some women'll put out anywhere."

Hot, angry words quivered on Nora's tongue, urgent and heedless. Before she realized it, she'd taken several impetuous steps in their direction.

Stopping in front of the circle of men, Nora said to the cowboy, "Considering who's draped over you now, I guess you speak from personal experience."

The men around the stove erupted in laughter as Cissy stiffened, her face darkening as Nora's meaning hit home.

"Oh, I could never match you," Cissy spat out. "I don't have the stomach for sleeping with old men for money."

Nora stood before the group, aware of the men's avid, expectant gazes. They wanted a cat fight, and would obviously relish a brawl between the two women.

She should have known better than to have responded to their slurs. Nothing good could come of this kind of mudslinging.

Turning away, she walked quickly to the door as a swell of murmurs and snickers rose from the group.

"Nora." Hoyt's voice caught her as she grasped the handle.

She turned her head, struggling to keep her emotions off her face.

"I'll make sure and point out your announcement

to anyone who might be interested," he said. His eyes were kind, his compassionate gaze comforting.

"Thank you, Mr. Daniels," Nora said before pushing open the door.

Once outside, the chill wind gusted in her face like a slap. Nora caught her breath, an angry sob escaping her.

It wasn't fair! She'd done nothing to entice Richard's boss. If anything, she had tried to avoid the man!

Stewing over it didn't do any good. All she could do was grit her teeth and wait for the jackals to find fresh meat. But she'd show them. Some day her riding school would be the biggest thing in Stoneburg. She'd make it happen or die trying.

Chapter Three

The warm smell of horses and sweet hay filled the barn, warding off some of the chill in Nora's bones. Winter's return to North Texas had made a rough workout for her and Chessie this afternoon. She'd cut it short when the wind picked up, but not before heading out to the fields for a wild gallop that set her heart pounding.

Nora kept up a steady rhythm, brushing Chessie's coat in even strokes, focusing on her movements in hopes of ignoring the prickle of excitement that ran across her skin.

Every now and then, a clatter from the tack room reinforced her awareness of Bret's presence in the barn. He'd breezed in after she started working on Chessie, his brief greeting and tantalizing grin igniting a flurry of awareness in her.

She tried to dismiss the memory of the sensation of being in his arms, the rush of breathless passion his kiss brought. Unfortunately, her efforts weren't very successful.

The dim light in the stall seemed almost cozy, while the mare's breathing accompanied by the shifting sounds of animal life filled the barn. Blowing on her hands to try to warm them, Nora ignored the wind shrieking around the building.

This was where she felt the most peaceful, sharing a silent communication with a horse. Putting Chessie through her paces every day gave a structure, a purpose to Nora's time that far exceeded anything she'd gained from her days living with Richard.

A niggle of frustration tugged at her. How long would it take for the people of Stoneburg to accept her again? The scene in the feed store still grated on her nerves. She'd regretted responding to the taunts. It hadn't done any good and might have strengthened Cissy's determination to cause trouble.

The sound of the barn door opening broke into Nora's thoughts, and a rush of cold air swept into the building.

Nora glanced over her shoulder and spotted Eve struggling to tug the door shut.

"Nora?" her friend called out in an anxious voice, her brow furrowed as her eyes adapted to the dim light.

"Over here."

Eve tugged at her gloves as she walked over to Chessie's stall. "God, that wind is awful."

"A real blue norther. Come in and warm up."

The other woman stuffed her mittened hands into her pockets.

"How did Jessica feel about her lesson the other day?" Nora asked when Eve didn't say anything more.

"Good. Really good." She paused, a nervous expression on her face.

"Is something the matter?"

"No, I just dropped by to talk to you about a . . .

a change in our class schedule. I'm afraid we need
to postpone your visit to talk to the class.''

"Postpone?''

"Yes, we have a really busy schedule now. The TASP
test is coming up—''

"I thought you said that was later.''

"Well,'' Eve cleared her throat. "Yes. . . .''

Nora put the currycomb down on the post. "Eve?
Is there a problem with my coming to talk to your
class?''

Eve's face puckered. "I'm sorry, Nora. I'm really
sorry! Mr. Stewart, the principal, told me not to have
you come.''

"What? Why?''

Her friend looked down, catching her lip between
her teeth.

"Because of the gossip,'' Nora answered her own
question, her voice hard. "That's it, isn't it?''

"Yes. I'm really sorry.''

"I'm such a terrible person that he thinks I'll cor-
rupt little children just by talking to them about
riding?'' The thought sliced her to the quick. This
was too much.

"Oh, honey. You're not terrible.'' Eve placed her
hand over Nora's where it rested on the stall. "Stewart's just worried about his job. He's always been a
real suck-up.''

"Can't they see I'm not like that?'' Nora could hear
the hurt in her own voice as outrage flooded her.
"I'm not a witch.''

"I know,'' her friend said miserably. She glanced
nervously at her wristwatch. "I'm really sorry. I have
to go. Jessica's playing at a friend's house and I'm
already late picking her up. I just had to tell you
about this in person.''

Nora picked up the currycomb, her hand clenching on the handle.

"You're not mad at me, are you?"

Glancing up at her friend, Nora said quickly. "No, of course not. Go get Jessica. I'm okay."

Eve hesitated a moment longer. "I'll call you."

"Good." Nora turned away, combing Chessie's mane, holding her feelings in check to keep from further upsetting Eve.

"I'm sorry," Eve said again. "Bye."

"Goodbye." A moment later the barn door opened and slammed shut with a swirl of wind and hay.

Slumping against Chessie, Nora trembled with the anger that rushed in. Never had she believed it would go this far. Kids like Jessica were the reason she wanted to teach riding. How could anyone think she'd damage school children?

Instead of dying down, the gossip just seemed to be mushrooming. She had to face the possibility that it might even affect her being able to buy the Turner property. Mrs. Turner was one of the most upstanding women in town, the daughter of a former governor, the mother of the mayor of Stoneburg.

She'd been part of the group of women at the diner that day.

What were the chances that Mrs. Turner would sell her homestead to a hussy like Nora? It just wasn't fair! Nora sobbed beneath her breath, her hands shaking so badly she gave up trying to groom Chessie. The big horse shifted, tossing her head gently as she eyed Nora.

Leaving the stall blindly, she turned to slam her hand against the rough wall.

Bret heard a thud. There was no point continuing to look for the bridle. From the moment he'd turned his attention to the conversation between Nora and

Eve, he hadn't really seen the stuff on the table in the tack room.

He told himself it was rude to eavesdrop and even ruder not to let the fact be known, but he couldn't hide in here knowing how Nora must be feeling.

Pushing open the tack room door, he stepped into the barn and saw her slumped against the wall next to the mare's stall. Even from this distance, he could see that she was crying.

So much for staying out of it.

He crossed the cement floor to where she stood.

Nora stiffened at his approach, surreptitiously wiping at her cheeks.

"It's a real bitch, isn't it?" Bret made no pretense he hadn't overheard. "Here you are paying for something you never did."

That brought her head up. She studied him through narrowed eyes. "What do you mean?"

"All this gossip about you seducing Richard's boss."

Nora tilted her head. "You don't think I seduced him?"

Bret laughed softly. "No, I don't."

"Why not?" she asked bitterly. "Everyone else in town has tried me and found me guilty."

"The way I see it, not only are you too smart to play footsie with a guy on the side, you're also too honest." Bret couldn't say how, but he knew she'd never cheat on a man.

"Honest?"

He shrugged. "You just don't work that way. I could see Cissy doing something like that, but not you."

"Thanks." She straightened from the wall, her normally soft face still hard with anger.

"But the real problem," he went on, "is that you're letting people in town run over you."

"What?"

"All you need to do is show them who's boss and they'll leave you alone."

"How? By talking back when they say nasty things? I've tried that. It just stirs things up more."

"You have to convince them that you can't be kicked around."

"I can't imagine how I could do that," she said.

"See, Nora, it's not that you've supposedly done such a terrible thing. Most folks here in town have done worse or had worse done to them."

"So why are they tormenting me?" The words seemed wrenched from her.

" 'Cause you're letting them."

"What can I do about them having trashy minds?" She shoved away from the wall and paced in front of Chessie's stall.

"Well, for one thing," he said, "you can stop acting like a guilty woman."

Nora stopped. "I am not acting guilty!"

"You don't go out anywhere or do anything fun except with Eve and her family. Except when you're here, you hide in your mother's house. And when you meet people on the street, you march past them with hardly a smile."

"They've judged and condemned me! What am I suppose to do? Invite them over for tea?"

"Maybe not invite them for tea, but smiling at them is a good idea."

She stared at him, disbelief on her face. "You've got to be kidding. Me having a cheerful expression will make them change their minds about me?"

"Honey, you need to show them you don't care what they think about you. Show them you're not cowering in your room. You need to throw this stuff back in their faces."

"I don't have a clue about how to do that." She'd stopped pacing and he thought he saw a glimmer of interest in her eyes.

He smiled, ready to jump on the opportunity to help her out and maybe earn himself another of her kisses. "Go out with me tonight. We'll kick up our heels, drink and laugh."

Nora looked up at him, an arrested expression on her face. "Going out with you will show the town that I can't be run over?"

"It'll show them that you're not gonna be controlled by the talk. We'll go to the Roadhouse, have a few beers and dance till dawn." And maybe more, if his luck held.

"I can't go to a place like that," she gasped. "People will talk even more."

Bret shook his head. "It's just a bar, not a cathouse. Stop thinking like your mother."

"I am not my mother," she said distinctly. "Not that there's anything wrong with her."

"No, of course not," he agreed, privately amused at her response. "But refusing to go to a bar just because it used to be a little rowdy—that's something your mother would do."

"I probably shouldn't be seen with you on a date anyway," Nora said. "Your reputation is far from spotless."

"That's why I'm the perfect guy for the job," he claimed. "Going out with some goody-two-shoes guy would just look like you're desperate to reclaim your reputation. We've got to go show them that you don't care about what they're saying."

A small smile tugged at the corner of her mouth.

* * *

Nora looked in the mirror and swallowed hard. She had to be out of her mind. Why did insanity surface at the worst moments?

She'd been unbalanced three months before when she'd bought the dress on a rash impulse, and she was just as crazy this afternoon when she agreed to go out with Bret. She couldn't believe that she was actually wearing the thin red slip of a dress tonight. The woman in the mirror even had a bit of a wild-eyed look.

The soft silk slid over her body with loving faithfulness, snug around her breasts, smooth over her hips, stopping daringly at mid-thigh.

She drew in a rough breath. Whatever was she thinking? And what's more, how on earth did she propose to get out of the house wearing this? Her mother would have a heart attack.

The thought stiffened her backbone. She'd promised to go out with Bret tonight and she was determined to see it through.

She couldn't wimp out. There were too many things to prove . . . to the town scandalmongers . . . to Principal Stewart . . . and to herself.

Tired of getting pushed around, Nora felt decidedly defiant.

What was more, she had something to prove to Bret. It was his fault she was wearing the red dress for the first time. She couldn't let him think he affected her so strongly that she was afraid to be in his company.

And it wasn't as if they'd be alone for the whole evening, she reminded herself. How far could things go in a crowded bar?

Nora ran a nervous hand down the skirt of the dress. Bret Maddock was too darn sure of himself.

He was right about one thing, though. She had been holding back, waiting for the storm to blow over. Darn it, she hadn't done anything wrong. Why shouldn't she go out with an attractive guy?

She turned away from the mirror, her stomach quivering.

Because this particular man seemed to tap into something inside of her that she knew better than to give into. Bret made her want to be held, made her want to lean on him.

Even when she knew she shouldn't. Self-reliance kept a woman from finding herself at the mercy of a man's deceit.

But she'd committed herself to going out tonight. With Bret, of all people. The one man who awakened desires she'd never felt before.

She could control herself, and him, tonight. Would she be able to resist if Bret stormed her fortress? She had to be sure, had to reassure herself of her own strength, and so she'd accepted his challenge and upped the ante with the weight of one flimsy red silk dress.

The jangle of the doorbell jolted Nora from her thoughts. Snatching up her coat, she pulled it on and left the room.

Bret stood in the tiny front foyer, his tall, lean frame delectably encased in snug jeans with a starched shirt just visible inside his jacket.

Exchanging pleasantries with Bret, Sharon Hampton wore an uneasy smile on her face. Nora walked forward, eager to get beyond the house, outside the range of her mother's nervous disapproval and into the danger of the evening.

"Hi." Bret's smile sent shivers down her body.

"Hi," she returned, bolstering her guard against his charm.

"I hope you won't be out too late, Nora," her mother said doubtfully. "You know you need your rest."

"I'll be fine," Nora responded, moving toward the door.

"Good night, Sharon." Bret waved as he followed her out.

The cold night air engulfed them as they went down the sidewalk to a luxury sedan that waited at the curb.

"Whew! That woman's downright worrisome," he declared as he opened the car door for Nora. "Was she so concerned when Richard came to pick you up?"

Nora slid into the car with surprise. She'd just assumed that Bret always drove a truck. This vehicle's dash gleamed with all the latest electronic wizardry, almost looking like a cockpit of an airplane.

"Mother thought she knew Richard. You, she's less sure of."

Bret got into the driver's seat and started the car. "Mother doesn't approve of me?"

Nora looked down at her hands in her lap. "She would if she thought you were looking for a wife. Mother has her own ideas about redeeming my reputation."

"I see." He backed out of the drive. "Marriage isn't a bad idea, but it's a big step to take just to save your good name."

"I agree," Nora told him. "That's part of the reason I've been hiding in my room. To avoid her matchmaking."

"Well, you don't have to worry about that tonight." Bret flashed her a grin. "We're just gonna have fun."

They drove through the dark streets in silence. His words tumbling around in her head. He couldn't have said anything to better verify her opinion of him. Nothing serious, nothing long term. Bret was more honest than Richard.

Sitting there next to Bret, she felt acutely aware of him, his powerful body, the potent way he'd kissed her.

What a lover he'd make, if a woman was interested in a fling.

As he turned onto the highway that led to the Roadhouse, pictures flashed in Nora's mind. Bret making love to her till she gasped out his name. The thought left her with a trembling sensation in her midsection.

"Well, here we are." He pulled into the gravel parking lot that surrounded a huddle of shabby buildings. A garish neon sign flashed on a pole overhead.

Nora gripped her small purse, suddenly wondering why she trusted Bret enough to come tonight.

"Ready, honey?"

She jerked back to consciousness, realizing that Bret was holding her door open.

"This is it. Your declaration of independence."

Nora climbed out of the car and turned toward the building with a sense of defiance. Bret was right about one thing—she was darned tired of sitting at home.

The smell of cigarette smoke engulfed them when Bret opened the door, his hand at the small of Nora's back.

She took a few steps forward, waiting as Bret took her hand. The noise and smoke of the place pounded against Nora's senses. Everywhere she looked, people in western wear crowded at tables that surrounded a scarred dance floor.

Bret threaded his way through the crowd to an empty table. A band was playing country music with a sexy, swaying beat and the twang of a guitar. She sat in the chair Bret held out for her.

Inside, the dilapidated building wore shadows. Men in cowboy hats and women in tight jeans moved on the dance floor. Light sparkled off the raised platform on which the band played.

On one side, an open arch revealed a pool room. A woman leaned over the first table, a pool cue in her hand, her breasts threatening to spill out of her tight sweater. Glancing around surreptitiously, Nora's fears were confirmed.

The place was a meat market. In the dead of winter, at least three nymphets on the dance floor were wearing cutoff shorts brief enough to threaten imminent exposure. Another woman sported a western shirt with deep fringe and strategic cut-outs.

"Let me take your coat, Nora."

Startled, she glanced up to see Bret standing by her chair.

The moment of truth.

Slowly, she stood, her fingers struggling with the belt on her coat. What had she been thinking when she wore this dress?

Knowing she didn't have a choice, Nora opened her coat and let it fall off her shoulders. As she did, another thought hit her. What if Bret didn't even notice the dress?

Glancing over her shoulder at him, that fear evaporated.

Bret stood looking at her, a stunned expression on his face.

"You . . . ah . . . really got into the spirit of this." He seemed to tear his eyes from her silk-clad body, fastening them on her face. "If anything will show the gossips that you aren't afraid of them, it's that dress."

Nora abruptly sat down again, resisting the urge to huddle lower in her chair. Bret tossed her coat into a chair along with his and sat next to her.

"Can I take your order?" A denim-clad and booted waitress appeared beside them.

Bret looked at Nora, his eyebrows raised.

"Anything." It didn't matter since she couldn't swallow.

"Two beers," he told the girl with a smile.

When she'd disappeared through the crowd, Bret leaned forward and picked up Nora's hand from the table. His fingers felt strong and calloused against hers.

"So tell me again why this is a good idea," she challenged, her stress bypassing years of ingrained politeness.

His thumb caressed the back of her hand, sending warmth over her skin with the speed of light. He leaned closer, pitching his voice so she could just hear it over the music. "You're here to show them you're not letting them run your life."

A shiver of awareness rippled through her at his closeness. "Right. Like I've done such a good job of it so far."

Bret laughed, throwing back his head. "Honey, you won't get any complaints from me."

"It's just the dress," she said dismissively, beginning to enjoy the conversation. Sitting here at the table with Bret so close, it seemed as if they were alone together in the crowd.

"Nope." He shook his head, a gleam in his eyes. "A dress only showcases the woman, and I've never seen one do it so well."

"Thank you," she murmured, wishing her drink

had arrived. Even the nasty taste of beer would be better than this dryness in her mouth.

This was why she'd worn the dress. She wanted Bret to look at her like that, had wanted him to for weeks. It was amazing how having her wish come true could be both exhilarating and frightening at the same time.

Bret stood up. "Let's dance."

Never had the red dress seemed so brief. Nora felt like she was wearing neon. They reached the edge of the dance floor too soon. Unfortunately, it was not crowded enough for them to lose themselves there.

"I haven't done much country and western dancing," she confessed as he pulled her to him.

"No problem," Bret said, taking her into his arms.

For some reason, being wrapped in his embrace felt different, more intimate than when she'd danced with all those businessmen Richard had entertained.

Nora inhaled his scent and told herself to relax. The steps seemed simple enough. She'd always been a good dancer, but she just couldn't lose herself to the music as they circled the dance floor. With Bret's hand warm on her back, the print of his palm seem to burn through the thin material, hot against her skin.

Staring over his shoulder in a daze, she felt his every movement, the rub of his fingers against the silk of her dress, and wondered if she'd ever feel Bret's hands on her bare body.

Bret wondered if he'd lost his mind. Never had red silk packed such a punch. When he'd suggested this date to Nora, he'd anticipated enjoying her company, even harbored a faint, dishonorable hope that she'd fall into his arms, maybe his bed. But he'd never expected her to show up looking this fabulous.

He could feel the tension in her body, even though she moved in spontaneous response to the music.

She'd surprised him when she'd agreed to go out with him tonight, but despite her reservations about this course of action, the woman had taken him at his word and thrown herself into the endeavor. He just hoped he didn't end up drooling all over her.

Of course, it would help if he could lower his body temperature seven or eight degrees. Asking her to dance hadn't been the brightest move.

When the song was over, they ended up on the far side of the dance floor. Bret had half turned to head back to their table when the band broke into a bunny hop.

All around them couples were hooking up in choo-choo style, their feet keeping rhythm with the steps. On impulse, Bret caught Nora's hand and pulled her into the line. Not wanting anyone else's hands on her waist, he got behind her himself.

With each kick-step, kick-step, hop-hop-hop, her fanny wiggled to the music. Bret could barely keep from stumbling over his own feet. As they bunny-hopped their way across the dance floor, Nora threw back her head to look at him, laughter breaking over her beautiful face. He found himself laughing with her.

Kick-step, kick-step, hop, hop, hop. He heard her giggling as they went, her tension dissolving in the foolish dance.

Bret's feet went on auto-pilot as he tried to remember the last time he'd heard anything more arousing than her laughter.

When the music ended, they were breathless.

Nora tossed back her tumbled hair and smiled up at him. "That was fun."

"You bunny hop like a pro," he teased, leading her off the dance floor.

"Years of experience," she said. "Can't you see Richard hopping around a dance floor?"

He couldn't help but chuckle at the image.

Nora's smile widened. Standing at the edge of the dance floor in the noisy, smoky bar, she looked beautiful. Her face glowed with the exertion of the dance and relaxed laughter. Every hint of the cool, self-possessed woman she usually was seemed to have evaporated.

Meeting her eyes, he felt a twinge of emotion he couldn't identify, something warm and gentle that centered in his chest.

"Want to play pool?" he blurted out.

"Pool?" She looked doubtfully toward the pool room. "It looks kind of crowded."

"Come on," he grabbed her hand, "we'll find a table."

The pool room seemed quiet after the band's noise. Towing Nora past the first row of tables, Bret found an open table in the back.

"You hold the table, I'll go get us set up," he told her.

When he returned a few minutes later, he found her eyeing the game at the next table as an attractive silver-haired man lined up a shot.

Bret started racking up the balls.

"I hate to sound like a broken record," Nora said, "but I haven't played pool in a long time. I'm not sure I'll remember."

"No problem," Bret assured her. "There's only one basic rule as far as you're concerned. If you have to make any shots where you stretch over, make sure your back is to the wall."

She looked down at her brief skirt and giggled. "I'll remember that. Now aren't we supposed to do something with the little round things on the table?"

The next half hour was grueling for Bret. How could he have thought this would be better than dancing? He'd never before realized that teaching someone to play pool could be considered a contact sport.

"Okay," he said, standing back. "Those are the basics. Take your best shot."

Nora positioned herself and sent the cue ball rolling across the table's green surface to thud into the pack. When the nine ball kept rolling and, totally by luck, fell into the far pocket, she raised her cue stick and cheered.

By some off chance, her next shot sent the three into the side pocket. This time Bret cheered.

Three shots later, they were drawing the attention of the tables around them and he was beginning to think he'd been hornswoggled.

Bret hooked his fingers in his pockets and stood watching her.

Who'd have guessed that sweet little Nora could play pool like a shark?

This game was taking on a whole new level of excitement. He couldn't help but itch to discover her other hidden talents.

Chapter Four

Two more balls rolled across the table, settling into pockets. By the time a third banked off the side and ended up in the corner pocket, play had stopped at the three tables around them, and a small crowd had gathered, drawn by Nora's little cries of triumph.

Bret leaned on his pool cue and glared at the woman gracefully poised over the table.

When the last ball dropped and their impromptu audience cheered, Nora straightened and turned toward him, an excited sparkle behind the too-innocent look in her eyes.

"Whew, she beat you bad," volunteered a guy from the next table, pushing back a battered cowboy hat.

Leaning his own cue against the table, Bret grasped hers and brought it up as a barrier between them. She smiled demurely, her hands bracketed between his on the cue.

"Nora Elizabeth, you lying woman," he said. "You must have played pool when you were in diapers."

Her laugh was low, a husky sound that traveled

through him like a heat wave. "All I said was that I hadn't played in a long time, and that's true."

"I'd say you got hooked up with a shark," suggested the silver-haired man who'd been playing with the cowboy. He smiled at Nora. "You thinking about turning pro, ma'am?"

She smiled back, her face glowing with accomplishment. "I don't think I'm quite that good."

The man looked vaguely familiar to Bret, which wasn't surprising since the Roadhouse pulled customers from all the surrounding area.

"I have to agree with your friend," the older man said. "You play like you grew up in pool halls."

Nora laughed, shaking her head ruefully. "Thanks, but it was partly luck. I haven't touched a cue since college, and even then only played on a dusty table in the dorm basement."

"We've got such lousy players around here, like poor Wyatt," the stranger gestured toward his partner in the battered hat. "You could probably earn your livin' off them."

"Jake!" the cowboy protested. "I ain't that bad."

"Well, I'm not a pool shark," Nora jumped in. "I'm a riding instructor. I'm setting up an equestrian academy in Stoneburg."

Bret glanced at her in surprise. She was loosening up nicely. If she kept moving in this direction, the woman wouldn't have any trouble convincing people she meant business.

"Equestrian? That's English style riding, isn't it?" the stranger asked.

"Yes." The question seemed to dim her excitement a shade. "Some people think Western is the only way to ride, but equitation and dressage are very beneficial in helping kids learn discipline and good horse care."

The older man smiled kindly at her, his humorous

gaze touching Bret's for an instant. "Folks around here can get stuck in their ways. You'll probably have to put dynamite under some folks to get them to think different."

"That's not a bad idea," she agreed, smiling.

"Sounds like time to change the direction of the conversation," Bret said, taking the cue out of Nora's hands. He snagged her hand and led her around the table. "Let's dance."

"It was nice talking to you," she called out to the older man as Bret towed her toward the dance floor.

"You, too, ma'am."

"Hey, Bret!" a man called out as they made their way to the dance floor. "You gonna win the Riding Club Championship again this year?"

"I'm giving it my best shot," Bret said, not stopping.

"Let me buy you a beer," the guy offered.

"Thanks." Bret smiled. "Maybe later."

The dance floor was more crowded now, the air smokier. He cradled Nora to him, not minding the close quarters.

"The guy in the pool room was nice," she said as they danced.

"Very nice. Most people around here are," Bret reminded her. "You've got to help them get to know you."

"I grew up here," she said with asperity. "The worst of the gossips have known me since I was born."

"No," he disagreed gently as he smoothed the tumble of hair away from her cheek. "They knew the quiet Nora Hampton who lived here half the year and in Wichita Falls half the year. But you've got to help them see this Nora, the grown-up woman who wears sexy dresses and plays dirty tricks on her pool partners."

She stared up at him, her eyes struggling to see in

the smoky darkness. "Ruffling people's feathers isn't a good way to start a business. I came tonight because I was mad at Principal Stewart."

"Whatever the reason," he whispered, drawing her closer against his body, "I'm glad you're here."

Bret lowered his mouth to hers. She tasted like red silk, warm and soft and hungry, her mouth clinging to his. A bolt of piercing need shot through him. He angled his mouth over hers again, sampling her dampness, aching to taste all of her.

In his arms, she felt like every dream he'd ever had, soft against his hardness, erotically curved and pliable. He slid his hands down her back, savoring the feel of her through her flimsy dress. His fingers detected the thin restraint of her bra strap and his mind envisioned her bare breasts cupped in his hands.

Lifting away from her lips, he heard her gasp as their bodies came into full contact. He was only dimly aware of the bar full of people and the shuffling, crowded dance floor.

Nora pulled back slightly, her face soft with lingering passion, her eyes dazed. She glanced around as if only then becoming conscious of their surroundings.

"I need to leave," she gasped.

"Afternoon, ma'am." The ranch hand tipped his hat as he and Nora passed in the barn door.

"Afternoon," she responded, grateful that some people maintained their courtesy regardless of gossip. In the face of the talk about her, she'd dealt with innuendo and outright propositions from some men in town. But the hands who worked at the Maddock ranch had always been polite.

Taking off her riding helmet as she stepped into

the sunny February day, Nora stopped a moment to let her eyes adjust.

It wasn't until she turned toward her car that she noticed the woman in the white Mercedes coupe. Parked next to Nora's economy car, the expensive sports car gleamed with a high polish.

The woman getting out of the Mercedes wasn't quite so highly glossed, but she had that undefinable aura of prosperity.

She didn't seem much over twenty-five, her blond hair looking natural and chic and her clothing casual.

Nora started across to her own car, curious but not wanting to stare.

"Excuse me," the woman called out.

"Yes." Nora's steps faltered.

The other woman smiled, the friendly gesture enlivening her attractive face. She came forward, offering her hand. "I'm Melanie Lockhart. Are you Nora Hampton? I'd like to talk with you about riding lessons for my daughter."

Excitement bubbled through Nora. "Oh! Of course. Nice to meet you, Mrs. Lockhart." With the rock that gleamed on the woman's finger, she didn't have to guess about her marital state.

"I'm glad to meet you, too, Nora. Please call me Melanie."

"Thank you, Melanie. How old is your daughter?"

The other woman smiled. "She's eight, and she has more energy than I know what to do with."

Nora nodded. "Learning proper riding technique is an excellent way to channel high spirits."

"Sounds wonderful," Melanie said ruefully, "because I'm almost worn out from keeping up with her. Her father is the one who suggested that riding might help. I don't know if you'll remember him, but he said he saw you whip the pants off Bret Maddock at pool the other night."

Nora felt as if she'd turned to stone. "Oh. Yes. I—I did." This gorgeous woman couldn't be married to the cowboy in the battered hat, but that left only the silver-haired man. The other observers couldn't have known about her teaching riding.

"Jack was very impressed with your pool playing abilities," Melanie said humorously. "He said anyone who could handle a guy the way you handled Bret Maddock could probably make sure that Lyssa stays out of trouble."

Apparently, Jack hadn't seen the kiss on the dance floor or he might have been more concerned about the way she'd "handled Bret."

"Well," Nora managed a weak smile, "I'll certainly do my best. How did your husband know how to find me?"

The other woman shrugged. "I guess he asked around about the riding academy." She looked around. "You're finished with lessons for the day? Or don't you give them on Mondays? I hope I'm not bothering you on your day off."

"Not at all." Nora hesitated. "I'm really just getting the academy started."

"Of course." Melanie smiled. "I'll pay for the first month."

"Fine." Nora's conscience stabbed her as the other woman drew out her checkbook. Jack and Melanie Lockhart were nice people. Did they know about the scandal? Surely, he'd have heard about it from whoever told him where to find her.

For weeks, all she'd wanted was to find people who didn't know about the gossip and get them to sign their children up for lessons. And here she stood about to acquire a student well able to afford a year of lessons, and she found herself battling with the sensation that she was deceiving this friendly woman.

"Mrs. Lockhart—Melanie," she blurted out. "I think you should know that part of the reason I don't have more students is that there's been some . . . talk . . . about me in Stoneburg."

The other woman looked up from the check she was writing, a faint smile on her face. "Really? Did you rob a bank?"

"No! Nothing like that," Nora gasped. "My former fiancé claims I was unfaithful—"

"Oh, that kind of talk." Melanie handed her the check.

"Nora, I'm married to a rich man who's twenty-four years older than me. Gossip no longer scares me."

"Uh, thank you." Embarrassed, Nora took the check.

"I tell you what," Melanie suggested. "If you won't believe that I married Jack for his money, I won't believe whatever your fiancé says about you."

Nora smiled tremulously. "Thanks."

After agreeing on lesson times, Nora watched the woman get in her car. Still in shock from the turn of events, she could hardly believe her luck. Even with the check in her hand.

The Mercedes backed out and headed down the drive, passing Bret's truck as he pulled up to the gravel area outside the barn.

Nora watched the white car disappear. If she hadn't gone to the Roadhouse with Bret, she'd never have met Jack Lockhart.

Maybe defiance had its reward after all.

"Who was that?" Bret slammed the truck door.

Nora turned, a silly grin taking over her face. "The

mother of my newest student," she declared saucily, "and the wife of our friendly pool-playing stranger."

"Really?" Bret looked down the road.

"Yes. He was Jack Lockhart. Do you know him?"

"I know of him," Bret admitted. "I thought he looked familiar the other night."

"I didn't recognize him at all and I have no idea what made him decide on riding lessons for his daughter, but I'm deeply grateful." She carefully tucked the check in her pocket.

"From what I've heard, Lockhart moves in big money social circles, but he's a downhome kind of guy. I bet you'll be getting referrals from other social-ite mothers who want a classy activity for their kids," Bret predicted with a smirk.

"I hope so," Nora said. "I know you think English riding is only useful for social climbing. Go ahead and sneer. I don't care. This is my first real break and I'm thrilled."

"I never said it wasn't useful," he said. "If nothing else, you brighten the scenery in those riding pants. I'm just not sure that your average Texan is gonna sign up."

"Then I'll have to attract above-average Texans," she retorted, turning toward the barn.

"An excellent plan," Bret agreed, falling into step with her. "Say, how about we take a celebratory ride to mark the occasion of your first big break?"

Nora glanced at him. "Don't you ever work?"

"Of course," his voice was wounded, "come spring round up, I'll be so busy directing men that you'll hardly ever see me."

"I'll believe it when I don't see you."

"So how about the ride?" he pushed.

She looked at him. The urge to go and wallow in his presence felt almost like a physical need. Although he presented a risk to her peace of mind, her feelings about him were changing. Not only did she feel the edginess of her attraction, she also felt, at some basic level, peculiarly safe. A feeling of rightness settled over her spirit whenever he was near.

Why not go riding? temptation whispered in her ear. *Nothing bad happened after the last time you went with him.*

"I don't know," she said. "I've been wondering since the other night if being seen with you is damaging for my reputation."

"How can you say that, woman?" His eyes danced in contrast to the shock on his face. "I'm the reason your luck has turned."

"Maybe so," she conceded. "And maybe the gossips are burning me in effigy. I haven't really gone anywhere over the weekend to see if I'm even allowed in town."

"Naw." Bret hooked an arm around her shoulders. "You're home free now. Just stick with me."

Nora laughed. "Jumping from the frying pan into the fire."

"Yeah." His arm tightened around her. "But fire can be so nice and hot. Come ride with me."

"Well," she weakened, battling her own urges and the exhilaration of his nearness, "maybe for a short ride."

Nora's heart fluttered while she saddled Chessie. Hearing Bret whistling as he readied his horse, she decided to go with the moment. Just this once, she'd let herself revel in a golden afternoon with the man of her fantasies by her side.

They were unlikely to be seen and if they were, it couldn't do much more damage to her wary heart. As long as she remembered that fantasies had their place, she'd be fine.

Leading the horses out of the barn, they mounted up and rode down a hard-packed dirt road that wound beside the ranch house and then away into pasture land.

Last week's blue norther had drifted to the south, leaving them with pale blue skies and sun-warmed earth.

"Steady, boy." Bret held his impatient mount with a firm hand.

"I guess you haven't taken General out for a run lately," Nora commented. "He's full of energy."

"He had a good gallop yesterday. He just tests me every now and then," Bret replied as the horse settled down. "So, are you ready to go dancing with me again? Give me a chance for a rematch at pool when I'm not in a state of shock?"

A giggle escaped Nora. Never had she hoped to use her innocently acquired ability to such good.

"I'm sure you could beat me if you were prepared," she said demurely.

Bret's laughter rang out, causing Chessie's ears to twitch in his direction. Nora kept the reins steady in her hand, empathizing with the horse's reaction. Bret's laugh frequently caused various parts of Nora to tingle.

They turned west as the road dwindled into a pair of tire ruts across open pasture dotted with scrub brush. An easy silence descended on them, broken only by the creaking of their saddles and the occasional jingle of the bridles.

Birds fluttered in the brush along the fence line, rising in a flurry of wings as the horses neared. The fields showed yellow in the sun, the whisper of winter weeds moving in the breeze.

"Want to do a little exploring?" Bret asked, stopping General at a broken spot in the rustic fence. "I don't think old lady Turner would mind if we just look around."

Nora shifted Chessie's reins. "You don't think she'd care?"

"Naw," he clicked softly to his horse, "besides, it's always easier to get forgiveness than permission."

"Sounds like your life motto," commented Nora, following him through the gap in the fence.

Bret grinned. "Works as good as any. Come on, we'll inspect the buildings."

Excitement thrummed in Nora's veins at the thought of showing him her dream. "Most of the acreage is west of here, isn't it?" she asked, trying to maintain her equilibrium.

He slanted her a glance. "You've decided to buy the place and you don't know the lay of the land?"

"I'm mostly interested in the house and barns," Nora replied. "Although I will need some pasture land."

"Well, you're right. The biggest part of the property lies west of the house. You can see the stock tank over there. I think there are one or two others in the far pastures." The brim of his hat dipped as he nodded toward the western horizon.

A cluster of farm buildings came into sight as they crossed the open field. Nora studied the simple white house huddled beneath a grove of oaks. There was nothing grand about the house or barn, but something about the homestead called to her. It was a feeling so personal she'd never been able to explain it.

"So this is it," Bret said as they skirted the corrals around the barn. "Your Shangri La."

"Yes," she retorted firmly, knowing he was seeing the place in comparison to the well-kept Maddock spread. Even before the years of neglect, this small ranch didn't compare to Bret's.

He halted his horse with a low-spoken word. "So tell me what you have in mind."

"I'll show you." She dismounted eagerly and looped Chessie's reins loosely around a corral post.

Bret followed suit and walked with her.

"It's not as large as the set-up you've got," she admitted, "but the barn's in good shape. I'd have two riding rings outside and build a small indoor working arena later." Nora pointed to the left of the barn, the new building clear in her mind.

"What about the house?"

"It looks like it'll need some updating, but I'm sure it's livable." The thought of having a place to herself, any place, made her feel warm and comfortable.

"Have you been inside?"

"No," she said. "I just peeked through the windows, but they're big enough to give me a good idea of how it looks."

"You've got lots of ideas," he said, as they walked around to the front of the house.

Bret tried not to look discouraging as they stood on the cracked sidewalk, surveying the dilapidated building. He could practically feel Nora's excitement about the place. Her voice held a vibrancy when she spoke about her plans, her face glowing with enthusiasm. All Nora had to do was breathe, and shivers went through him.

The house, on the other hand, made him tired just looking at it. Nora couldn't have any idea of how much work it needed.

Winter honeysuckle framed the porch, its tall, shrubby shape dotted with small dirty-white blooms. From this angle, he could see three broken windows and a roof that sagged ominously. How on earth could one woman take this on?

"Nora, honey," he said. "Have you thought about what you'll do if you don't get the riding school thing off the ground?"

She glanced up at him swiftly, a challenging light in her eyes. "I'm going to make a go of this."

Taking her arm, he turned her gently toward him. "Sometimes things don't work out the way we plan. It's not anyone's fault. You've got to be able to see other possibilities."

"No," she declared, turning away from his grip to stalk up to the porch. "I know the academy will be a success if I can get beyond the gossip." Nora sat down on the front porch, her oval face transformed into a picture of determination.

"It's not just the gossip," he said softly. "You're fighting an uphill battle to get folks around here interested in paying to learn how to ride a horse. They grew up riding."

She shook her head, her dark hair spilling over her shoulders. "If I can get beyond the stuff about Richard and convince Mrs. Turner to sell me this land, I'll make a go of it. I'm just afraid all the talk will keep her from selling to me."

A niggle of guilt tugged at Bret. In the beginning, it hadn't seemed necessary to tell Nora about his plans for the Turner property. He hadn't thought she'd go this far with the riding school. But standing here with her now, his body half aroused by her presence, he was beginning to see problems ahead.

All her dreams were tied up here. She had her heart set on having her riding school in this exact spot. Stealing land out from under a woman wasn't the way to win her over.

Not that she really had any claim on the property.

He'd seen it first and had already put out feelers about buying the place for a landing strip complete with a hangar. Its proximity to his family's ranch house and his cabin made it perfect.

Bret had no doubt that the old lady would listen to the recommendation of the guy who handled her finances. Fortunately, he and Jim Carlyle went back a long way.

"You know, honey. This isn't the only piece of land hereabouts." Bret sat down next to her on the top step.

"This is where I belong." Nora threw her arms wide. "It feels right. I can see myself living very happily here."

Her perseverance felt like a stone on his chest. "Why did you come back here, Nora, where Richard has such influence? You could have gone anywhere to start your school."

She shrugged. "When I first came home, I didn't realize what Richard had told his parents. It never occurred to me that anyone would think I'd tried to seduce his boss."

"But now," Bret pursued. "Why are you staying now? People have been so nasty I'd think you couldn't wait to leave."

Her moving away would make things so much easier. Not too far away, but out of Stoneburg where she faced such unfair treatment and where the land they both wanted could end his hopes for winning her.

What had started as a casual pursuit was fast taking on larger proportions. Bret wasn't totally sure what all he wanted with Nora, but he knew he wanted her in his life.

"I don't know," she sighed. "My mother refuses to move away. And Stoneburg is home. I never realized how much so until I lived in Dallas."

Sitting close like this, her scent drifting over him, Bret longed to touch her, to slide his hand beneath the weight of her hair and pull her to him. "Not much of a homecoming."

"I don't know how to explain it," Nora said. "It just seems like I have to stay. Not run away from this. Sticking it out here, starting the academy—I feel like I have to do it."

A restless wind teased the trees above them, scattering sunlight like a fall of golden confetti. Bret plucked a weed from the overgrown bed beside the steps, twisting the stem.

He'd wanted her to stand up to the gossips. Sitting next to her, watching the play of expressions on her face, he realized that Nora was taking a stand just by staying in Stoneburg.

Unthinking, he reached for her, sliding his arms around her slim shoulders. She looked up, her face tilted for his kiss.

In all his years, no woman had tempted him more. He felt drawn to her in ways he couldn't explain. When his lips met hers, the thunder of his heart became a roar in his ears. It was always like this with her, this sudden burst of hunger and urgency consuming him, primal urges surfacing faster than he could contain them.

He felt her hands clutch at him, a small reflexive movement. She tasted like honey, the stroke of her mouth like velvet beneath his. The scent of her, her bewitching body pressed against his, conjured heaven and hell.

It was too much for him, too much to expect him to let go of her. They'd sort out the details later. Now he needed the feel of Nora around him, beneath him, needed her more than air.

Chapter Five

He tasted of heat and sunshine and wicked, wonderful things. Nora leaned in for his kiss, the swirl of doubts and anxieties in her head dissipating with the rising tide of desire.

Her hands clutched at his broad shoulders, steadying her against the whirlwind of their kiss. Sensation shivered through her with the brush of his lips and she opened her mouth without hesitation, clung to him without thought. Nothing felt more natural than losing herself in the warm earthy scent of him.

She heard him murmur, a low hungry sound as he gathered her closer, lifting her up onto the porch until she lay against him.

This was a new thing, this sense of merging with a man until she wanted nothing but him. Nora trembled with the urgency of it, driven to hold the mating of their mouths.

He held her cradled in the crook of his arm, his damp, urgent mouth dropping to the curve of her neck, his hand cupping her hip to draw her closer.

Nora whimpered. Every part of her bloomed for him, aching for his touch. She moved against him, hunger thrumming in her. The sound of his ragged breathing mingled with the roar in her ears and she gasped as his hand trailed up her body to surround her breast. Bret took her mouth in a rough assault, the arc of his body hard against hers.

Kiss melted into kiss until Nora felt on fire, writhing against him and arching for his touch. His hand lingered on her breast, stroking her gently through her shirt until she could no longer think, craving the feel of him against her bare skin.

She lay back panting when he lifted from her mouth, his hands fumbling with the buttons of her shirt. When he brushed back the fabric, she trembled for the heat of his mouth against her. In a tangle of sleeves and arms, he did battle with the clasp of her bra until it came free, baring her to his touch.

Bret knelt above her, his face ablaze with desire, his hands stroking her flesh as if he'd found gold. He bent to nuzzle her, his breath hot and damp against her skin.

She lay on the porch, her hands caught in the tousle of his hair as he fondled and kissed her breasts. Each caress and suckle of his mouth drove her higher, tighter, hungrier.

In the back of her mind, caution cowered, held at bay by the ferocity of her need for him, the full, bright moment of fantasy come to life. And it was better— better than her dreams.

Yes, he was reckless, wild and undependable. But she'd been empty and cold for so long, had denied herself for so long.

Shifting, Bret knelt on the top step between her bent knees. He laved and suckled her breasts, his rock hard body inciting a riot of sensation despite the layers of clothes between them.

Dazed, Nora stared up at the ceiling of the porch, the cool air sharp against her heated skin. She felt herself moving against him, felt the thundering of her blood as she raced toward the cliff.

Her mind was a jumble, a frenzy of urgency. And yet, some part of her balked, pulled back on the reins.

This was Bret holding her in his arms, loving her like the devil's most proficient artisan. Reckless, risk-taking Bret, who'd never been true to one woman. *How could she trust him? He was a man and, by nature, a fickle one.*

He lifted from her breast, straining forward to capture her lips, his pelvis rocking against hers. Nora's mind disappeared in an explosion of fireworks, rivulets of pleasure showering her. The snap on her jeans popped free beneath his searching hands.

Nora bolted upright, her movement sending Bret rocking back on his heels.

"No," she gasped, groping for her discarded bra.

Balanced on the porch steps in front of her, Bret's breathing was labored, his hand outstretched as if to steady her.

"I'm sorry," she babbled. "I . . . we, I let it go too far."

"Hold on, sweetheart," he managed, his voice still rough with passion.

Nora fought the tears welling in her eyes as she awkwardly scrambled into her clothes. She'd never felt lower, never been so ashamed of herself. It was bad enough to allow herself to be this foolish, but to lead Bret on and then to stop him made her feel like a tease. She fumbled with her shirt. "I'm sorry."

"Nora, honey." He slid onto the porch next to

her, tugging her into his arms. "It's okay, sweetheart. Nothing happened."

"This is nuts. I should never have let you kiss me. I didn't mean to ... tease." She wrenched herself out of his arms, unwilling to be in such tempting proximity.

"Honey, don't give yourself grief." Humor laced his voice as he gave her a crooked smile. "I'm always hotter than a tamale when you're around."

"I didn't mean to let things get so carried away," she said again, struggling to tuck in her shirt.

"Well, there's where you're better than I am," Bret confessed. "I've been meaning to get carried away with you for a long time."

She glanced up at him, profoundly disturbed by the glow in his eyes. "It's not a good idea."

He held her gaze, his dark eyes smoldering as he said softly, "Seemed pretty damn good to me."

Nora looked away, her heart rate revving irresponsibly. How could he look so desirable, kiss her like she was the only woman on the earth ... and still be such a *man*? Unreliable, intrinsically dishonest, incapable of putting a woman's needs before his own.

But it wasn't his fault he had the Y chromosome.

Finally, she said, "I don't need any complications."

His smile faded. "Is that what this is? A complication?"

The words sounded gentle, but she couldn't read his face.

Nora got up from the porch, thrusting suddenly nervous hands into her jeans pockets. "I've got plans that will require all my energy. I can't afford to get ... distracted."

"Distracted," Bret repeated the word as he leaned back, his elbows propped on the top step.

She looked away from the disturbing stretch of his

taut, muscled body. "I'm not going to deny that I find you very attractive. It's just that right now—"

"—you can't be bothered with love," he concluded, an edge in his voice.

"No, I can't." She turned to face him. "All my life I've tried to do right by people, to be responsible and fair. You might have noticed it hasn't gotten me far. Now, I'm putting my dreams first. I just don't have the energy for a man."

Bret looked at her, his emotions shut out of his normally open expression. "So even though you like me and I like you, you don't want to take this any further because kissing me takes too much energy?"

"It's more than kissing," she said, forcing the words out through a tight throat.

Bret got up from the porch, dusting off his jeans. "This isn't about your plans for the riding school. It's about Richard. You're scared of getting hurt again."

"Thank you, Dr. Freud," she said sarcastically, fighting off a wave of anger, sadness and frustration all mixed together. "I suppose I should just sleep with you for the hell of it."

He walked to where she stood, stopping inches away. She met his gaze without flinching.

"What I think," Bret said softly, "is that you've never really loved a man or let him love you. This thing with Richard bruised your pride and sent you home with your tail between your legs. I think you're running scared, Nora."

"And sex with you would prove something?" she demanded angrily. "Hot, torrid sex would cure my problem?"

"I don't know," he said, turning toward their horses, "but you've got to give your heart to someone if you're ever going to meet life halfway."

"Leaning on a man got me into the situation I'm

in," Nora declared, determined not to let herself cry. "Now I have to make my own way, my own life. I don't have any other choice."

"You always have a choice," Bret said, meaningfully. "There's no situation that can't be finagled if you work it right. Love isn't the enemy. Fear is."

Watching him turn and walk away, Nora fought against the jumbled mess in her mind. She'd been very clear on it all, ever since leaving Dallas. If you put too much reliance on a man, you'd live to regret it. But now with Bret's words spinning in her head, she felt like she'd stepped into an alternate universe.

You've never really loved a man. . . . Hadn't she loved Richard? And what the heck was Bret up to? Men who just wanted a quick tumble didn't usually talk about love.

"Of course I'm not going to the Boys' Home Benefit," Nora declared. "Why on earth would I want to go to anything sponsored by the Riding Club? The worst gossips in town are on the Board."

Facing her friend Eve, Nora crossed her arms, determined not to allow her attention to stray toward where Bret was standing nearby. Even so, her peripheral vision faithfully reported his every movement as he lifted the saddle from his horse's back, the flex of his muscles evident through his shirt.

"Everyone goes to the benefit," Eve said, picking up a piece of paper that had drifted out of Jessica's open backpack.

"Here's your hat, Jess," Nora said, as the child trooped past on the way to her mother's car, her arms loaded with her backpack, sneakers and baseball mitt.

"I just think you ought to go," Eve persisted. "You

don't have anything to hide. The gossip seems to be dying down . . . despite your indiscretion."

"The benefit is the same every year," Nora retorted, ignoring Eve's comment. "Bad barbecue, Lex Martin's Rough Rider Orchestra and, this year, too many people who hate me. I can't see any reason why I should go."

"I can." Bret entered the conversation without preamble. "You should go to promote your business. If you're going to make your riding school work, you have to advertise it."

Nora swallowed hard, her entire treacherous body responding to the sound of his voice. In the last two days since their passionate clinch on the porch of the Turner house, she'd constantly battled her urges, remembered the feel of his touch—and thought about what he'd said.

"I have been doing some promoting," she said.

"Ask any small business person," Bret added. "You have to get involved in the community."

The thought of facing a roomful of accusing eyes didn't sound too appealing.

"Unless you're giving up on winning the town over." His words held a hint of a taunt.

"I'm not giving up. The scandal will blow over when everyone sees that I'm no different than I was when I grew up here."

"Then this will be the perfect opportunity to prove that to them, won't it?"

"So you're going," Eve concluded, her gaze bouncing avidly between Nora and Bret.

"With me," he said, his smile faintly challenging.

"No!" The word jumped out of Nora's mouth. "I'm trying to avoid gossip, not ask for it."

"You can come with us, Nora," Eve offered hastily.

                        * * *

The VFW hall looked the same as it always had
with its inadequate lighting and the scarred linoleum
floor. The band occupied the small stage area, the
aged musicians looking even more withered and cata-
tonic than the last time Nora had seen them.

Hesitating inside the doorway, she waited for Eve
and Tom. True, nothing drastic had happened after
her night at the Roadhouse, but she couldn't believe
the gossip had completely stopped. Of course, she
still hadn't been into town.

She glanced around, wondering if Bret had arrived
yet. It would be nice to have another friendly face,
even though this particular face had haunted her for
the last week. Maybe they could dance once without
arousing too much speculation. In her wildest
dreams, she couldn't imagine anyone else asking her.
At least not with their wives around.

Chattering people filled the room even though it
was still early. An unusually energetic buzz hovered
in the air, making Nora glance around curiously. The
Boys' Town Benefit had always been well-attended,
but she never remembered there being quite so many
people.

A few gray-haired couples ventured onto the dance
floor and were shuffling to the erratic rhythm of
the Rough Riders. The majority of the crowd stood
around the perimeter, watching.

"It's a pity your mother didn't want to come," Tom
remarked.

"She was tired," Nora repeated her mother's
excuse.

"Come on, Tom," Eve urged. "Let's get a table."

Nora followed them, aware of curious glances and
a strange wake of silence as they crossed the room.

A certain amount of that was normal these days, but there seemed to be an expectant gleam in the eyes of one or two people who met her gaze.

Across the room, Mrs. Turner sat at a table with several other older ladies. Nora smiled in their direction, hoping that Bret wouldn't single her out with Mrs. Turner here. Maybe there had been more talk about them than she'd realized.

Eve finally found a table that suited her and the three of them sat down.

"Chapparal Day is coming up," Tom commented jovially. "I hear the Riding Club is thinking about putting a handicap on Bret Maddock to give someone else a chance at winning the big race."

"It's about time," Eve said. "He's won that race for the last seven or eight years."

"Last ten years," murmured Nora, as she looked around.

Across the room, near Mrs. Turner's table, a large knot of people stood, the din of their voices loud enough to be heard above the music. As Nora glanced around, trying to look more comfortable than she felt, she saw Richard's mother break away from the group and hurry off to tend to some detail.

Although she hadn't said as much to Eve and Bret, Mrs. Worthington had figured largely in Nora's reluctance to come tonight. For as long as Nora could remember, Richard's mother had run the Riding Club.

A high-pitched giggle rang out, drawing Nora's attention back to the group in the corner. Cissy Burton. A trickle of anxiety ran down Nora's spine like the trail of a cold finger. Talk about walking into the lion's den.

Nervously straightening the dinnerware at her place, Nora told herself to relax and try to enjoy the evening. Surely, Mrs. Worthington and Cissy, also on the Riding Club Board this year, would be too busy to harass her tonight.

Eve's gasp pulled Nora's gaze up. Turning to see what drew her friend's reaction, she felt a sudden buzzing in her ears.

The cluster of people had shifted and through the opening, she saw Richard standing in the midst. Richard, her former fiancé, was here. A jumble of reactions crowded in her head. He'd never come back for the annual benefit when they'd been together. Had he seen her? How would he react to her presence?

"Omigod," Eve breathed. "I didn't know he'd be here."

"What? Who?" Tom stared around, clueless.

"Richard's here!" his wife hissed, elbowing him.

"I know," Tom said, his voice aggrieved as he rubbed the arm she'd hit. "I just thought you were talking about someone else."

"Who else would I be talking about?"

"It's okay," Nora soothed, trying to avoid drawing more attention to their table. "I'm sure he'll avoid me as much as I will him."

"Do you want to leave?" Eve asked anxiously.

Oh, boy, did she want to leave. "No," Nora said, drawing on a determination she didn't know she had. "I haven't done anything to be ashamed of."

She sure wasn't about to run scared. But try as she might to relax, the next half hour seemed to tick past slowly Eve directed Tom to bring them plates of food and Nora picked at the meal, moving the mound of barbecue around more than eating it. She forced herself to shift in her chair so she could see the rest of the room, unwilling to hide.

People still clustered around Richard in the far corner of the room. It was strange sitting here watching him. For years, she'd accompanied Richard to party after party. He was always after a new deal, making a new connection.

Nora sat, unwillingly transfixed by the scene. Her former fiancé stood surrounded by the elite of Stoneburg, entertaining them with his stories of business conquests. Even from this distance, she could read the situation. His stance presented him as a force to be reckoned with, and she knew that he practiced it.

He held center stage. It was admittedly a small stage, but she knew he'd be loving every minute of the attention. The hometown boy voted "Most Likely To Take Wall Street By Storm."

How strange to be here across the room from him, an observer to a play she'd once performed. Nora grappled with the emotions that surfaced in her—anger at his betrayal, sadness at the loss of their friendship, even a twinge of amusement. He looked so much like a rooster crowing over his domain.

They had shared something, some level of attachment, but it all seemed so long ago, as if it were another woman's life. Still, she couldn't understand why he'd tried so hard to hurt her.

The dance floor grew more crowded, couples were whirling past their table.

Nora shifted in her chair, suddenly feeling stifled. She felt closed in, chained by history and circumstance. For a wild moment, she wanted to race out of the building and launch herself into the air—to fly free from this town and everyone in it.

She remembered sitting high on the windmill tower, the wind swirling around her. No wonder Bret loved to fly. He got to leave all this behind.

"Do you want anything else, Nora?" Eve's voice jerked her back to the moment. "Tom's going back to the buffet. Do you want him to bring you anything?"

"No, I'm fine." She looked down at the napkin she'd been pleating and resisted the urge to scream.

"Care to dance, ma'am?"

Nora's gaze sprang up to meet Bret's.

He stood beside the table, a sight to behold in starched jeans and a turquoise western shirt with his cowboy hat tilted back on his head.

"Awfully nice music," he said, his eyes dark with the combination of an invitation and a dare.

"Do you think you ought to?" Eve asked nervously, her gaze darting around the room.

Nora glanced at the faces turned their way, suddenly conscious of the attention Bret's invitation had drawn.

"Remember," he said softly, "you're a business-woman with a goal. And you haven't done anything to be ashamed of."

A fluttering filled her midsection. Everything in her longed to get up out of her seat and twirl around the dance floor in Bret's arms.

Caution locked up her brain. "I don't think I—"

"Come on, Nora Elizabeth," he urged her. "Don't be afraid."

Was he talking about the gossip or something more, something just between them? Without conscious choice, she found her hand in his, the warmth and strength of his fingers drawing her up.

Bret led her to the dance floor, a smile blazing on his face. He swung her into his arms, the heat and scent of him settling over Nora like a drug.

The music shifted to a waltz, plaintive and graceful. As they circled the room, she fell into a rhythm that seemed familiar. Lifting her eyes to Bret's face, longing swamped her. She wanted him near, the charge of his presence wrapped around her, the rocketing sizzle of being in his arms.

She knew he packed a trouble more potent than Richard ever could, but still she wanted him. The starched cotton of Bret's shirt felt smooth and warm where her hand rested on his shoulder. Nora heard herself sigh as they slipped through the crowd on the dance floor, their steps as easy and natural as walking.

Leaning forward, he whispered, "Is this too involved, too close? I've never been a complication before. How am I doing?"

She looked up at him, feeling a sardonic smile curving her mouth. "You've always been a complication. Always."

A sudden smile brought a twinkle to his eyes. "Thank you."

Nora looked away, conscious of a swift pang in her chest. "Richard's here."

Bret bent forward, his lips brushing hers. "Who cares?"

She closed her eyes and swayed closer to him, not caring anymore. She'd protect her heart later.

"You dance like an angel, Nora," he murmured. He drew her closer, his hand warm on her back as he bent close to her ear. "Want me to punch Richard out for you?"

A startled laugh escaped her. "No!"

Bret sighed. "You sure know how to spoil a man's fun."

"No one spoils your fun for long," she retorted.

"Well, there are a couple of other things I'd enjoy more than popping Richard," he admitted, his eyes turning darker.

They dipped and glided, their feet light on the dusty floor as they floated past other couples. Every step matched as they drifted seamlessly around the dance floor, and even their hearts seemed to beat in rhythm. The Rough Riders Orchestra had never played so well.

Bret drew her arms up behind his neck. She knew she should protest. This was worse than dancing with him at the Roadhouse. Here, every eye in town watched them with avid speculation.

Nora rested her head on his chest, feeling the steady thump of his heart beneath her temple. Dancing with Bret was her reward for staying to face her accusers. At least here she couldn't succumb to her burning need to make love to him.

By the time they'd spun around the floor a few more times, Nora had lost track of Richard and his mother. The music ended with a flourish, and the Rough Riders stopped for a break.

Nora pulled out of Bret's arms, her caution back with a vengeance. "I need to . . . ahh . . . I'm going to check my makeup." She turned and slipped away through the crowd, needing a moment to herself to make sense of the emotions churning in her. She'd been attracted to Bret for weeks, but now he seemed to be invading her heart, and the thought sent her running for cover.

In the ladies' room, Nora washed her hands, patted her face with a damp towel and retouched the faint smudge of her mascara.

Every shred of common sense told her to retreat, to put as much distance between herself and Bret as was possible. Something about him short circuited her common sense.

Nora stepped out of the ladies' room and looked around. Eve and Tom had taken to the dance floor and were jogging around the perimeter in a dance move she couldn't identify.

When a swift survey of the room didn't reveal Bret's whereabouts, Nora turned toward the refreshment table. Barbecue simmered at one end of the table, but Nora headed for the iced soft drinks. One or two others were helping themselves to the potato salad and cole slaw. Nora picked up a can of soda, then turned to head back to the table.

Richard stood facing her, no more than a foot away, an expression of contempt on his face. Nora's heart hurtled into adrenaline overload and her throat constricted. But then her backbone stiffened. This was Richard, the man she'd planned on marrying, not some frightening ogre. As hurt and angry as she was, they'd still shared something she once thought was special.

She'd since discovered things about him that she hadn't recognized before. Like too many men, he was short on loyalty and ruthless in his need for advancement. His hostility toward her baffled Nora, but she wouldn't allow herself to scurry away.

"Hello, Richard," she said, her voice level.

"You certainly didn't waste any time finding yourself a playmate," he said, a sneer marking his handsome face. "Making a spectacle of yourself with Bret Maddock. What's the matter? Did you get tired of old men like Benson?"

"Richard." Nora glanced around, grateful that the serving area was deserted. "You know I wasn't involved with your boss."

He snorted in disbelief. "I used to think I knew you, Nora. Before you showed your true colors. Now I'm realizing how wrong I was. Do you know how much trouble you caused me with Benson? His wife was there, for God's sake."

"Please keep your voice down," she requested, aware of heads turning in their direction.

"I'm sure you'd like me to keep quiet," Richard declared, his tone more strident. "Although the way you were wrapped around Maddock out there on the dance floor, you might as well sell it on the street corner.''

Nora gasped, shocked at the vitriol pouring out of him. "You're crazy. Why are you saying these things?"

"What's the matter, Nora? Did you think you could keep your sleazy secrets here in Stoneburg?"

"You've lost your mind," she declared angrily.

"How long have you been playing around with Bret?" snarled Richard. "Did you sneak off to let him bed you every time we visited from Dallas?"

A crowd of onlookers had gathered in a semicircle behind Richard, their faces avid and shocked. Nora looked from one face to another, hoping to find one sane individual in the bunch. How could anyone who knew her believe these things about her?

Out of the corner of her eye, she caught sight of Mrs. Turner in the crowd. The woman's face was unreadable.

"I was totally faithful to you," she cried in frustration, feeling as if her dream of owning the Turner property was slipping through her fingers as she spoke.

"Yeah," he said scornfully. "Right up to when I found my boss with his hand up your dress."

An overwhelming sense of fury hit Nora. He didn't want to hear her, didn't want to believe her. There wasn't anything for her to say, nothing she could do to change this ugly, rending moment.

More than anything else, she wanted to hit him, to slap him silly, but one tiny sliver of sanity kept her from adding violence to her already tarnished reputation.

"Does Maddock do you better than I did?" Richard asked. "Doesn't he mind sharing you with other men? Or do you do it with more than one at a time?"

"What I do is no longer any of your business," she said in a hard voice. As she faced him, her body bracing to do battle, the crowd behind Richard seemed to shift and then split.

Bret strode forward, his tall, lean figure purposeful. Nora could hardly stifle the cry in her throat. Her hand lifted toward him as he crossed to her side.

Chapter Six

Bret's arm circled her shoulder, his face like granite as he met Richard's glare. "If you've got something to say, why don't we take it out to the parking lot?"

"I'm not afraid of a lowlife like you!" Richard huffed.

"You're the kind of crap that gets on a man's boots when he's not careful where he's walking. Why don't you come on outside and show me your morals?" taunted Bret.

Nora looked from one hostile male face to the other. How had this gotten so out of control? Richard's accusations made her furious, but she had to get out of this with some dignity.

"No, Bret." She tugged at his arm as he took a step toward Richard. "Let's just leave."

Bret stood unmoving for a moment, an expression on his face she'd never seen before. Gone was the lighthearted man who assaulted her better judgment at every opportunity. Nora could almost feel the danger emanating from him. Bret's eyes never left Richard's face. "He needs a lesson, honey."

She looked at Bret, her voice low, "Please."

"Are you sure?"

"Yes." She turned quickly toward the door, struggling to hold herself together until she could get away.

Bret followed her. She heard his bootsteps behind her on the hard floor. Stopping as the door closed behind them, she shivered in the chilly night air. Now she'd never convince Mrs. Turner to sell her the land.

A furious hopelessness clogged her throat. Why was Richard doing this? Why was he deliberately trying to hurt her? Nora gulped back a sob as she stood motionless on the pavement, only dimly aware of Bret's presence behind her.

In the front row of the crowded parking lot Richard's red sports car straddled two parking spaces, as if he'd felt entitled to take the extra room.

"I've got a pocketknife if you want to do his tires," Bret offered as he stood next to her.

Nora burst into tears.

"Come on," Bret said roughly. "Let's get out of here." He urged her toward his truck, a hand at the small of her back as she continued to sob into her hands.

He opened the truck door for her, then slammed it shut and walked around to the driver's side. In moments, they were roaring out of the parking lot.

Wiping her face with trembling, angry fingers, Nora wrestled her tears to a trickle. Bret drove in silence, the night engulfing them. When she shivered, he switched on the heater, sending a swirl of warmth around her legs.

Five minutes later, Bret turned off on a dirt road Nora didn't recognize. When they were well out of sight of the main highway, he turned into a drive that led to what looked like a log cabin.

Nora looked over at him in surprise, her eyes feeling hot from the tears.

"There's no way I'm taking you home to your mother like this," Bret declared as he switched off the headlights.

"Like what?" she whispered. She felt like a baby.

Opening the truck door, Bret ignored her question.

"What is this place?" She slid under the steering wheel and got out, staring at the building while he shut the door.

"My cabin. I built it myself. My living here instead of at the ranch house gives me and my parents some privacy."

"Oh." She followed him up the walk. "I'm really okay now."

"No, you're not." He opened the door and flipped on the lights. A leather couch and chairs sat on a woven rug of indeterminate color. Besides a small kitchenette in the corner, the only other feature of the room was a large screen television.

"You want some coffee?" He shut the door behind them.

"Thank you," she managed, his obvious concern bringing her close to tears again.

Bret sat next to her on the couch. "Honey, I've never known a woman with more reason to cry. Quit trying to hold it in. I've got a perfectly good shoulder here."

"I'm not crying," she snuffled.

"Come over here." Tossing his hat on a nearby chair, Bret reached out and took her in his arms.

"I'm not one of those women who cry all over the

place," she protested, sinking against him despite her determination not to give in to her tears.

"Just with me. Nowhere else. It's all right, honey," Bret whispered against her temple as he held her close.

Hot tears trickled down to drip from her chin. Nora tried to stem the flow, her efforts nearly bringing on the hiccups. Finally, she let the sobs come, embarrassed but unable to stop.

Bret held her, his body rocking ever so gently. He said nothing, didn't try to stop her or question her distress. Nora drew in a shuddering breath, the knot in her stomach loosening.

"I never expected him to be so nasty," she said abruptly, grappling to understand Richard's assault. "I thought he might refuse to talk to me—if only to please his mother—but to. . . ."

"You should have let me beat the bejesus out of him," Bret said, his hand gentle as he brushed away a lingering tear.

"That wouldn't have accomplished anything," she dismissed the idea. "And you might have gotten hurt."

"Excuse me?" He sounded more amused than insulted.

"I mean you might have hurt your hand or something when you hit him," Nora clarified, letting herself relax against him.

"It would've been worth it." His arms tightened around her.

Nora shook her head slowly, a sense of contentment starting to seep into her as she huddled in his arms. "This whole thing is so bizarre. I've been over it again and again, trying to figure out how I could have handled it differently. I had no idea that Richard's boss would behave like that."

"What did he do, exactly?"

She glanced up at Bret, realizing she'd never really talked to him about that pivotal night. "It was at Richard's New Year's Eve party. He gave one every year. I'd had the food catered but I was serving it myself."

"You and Richard lived together?" Bret asked.

"Yes," she said. "His boss, Mr. Benson, startled me in the kitchen that night. There were lots of people there from Richard's office, bigwigs above Benson."

Nora leaned her head back against Bret's arm where it rested on the back of the couch. "Of course, everyone was drinking. But Benson seemed completely sober. He just walked up, started kissing me and put his hands on my . . ." Her voice trailed off and she struggled not to shudder as the memory of the moment returned with shattering clarity.

"It's all right." Bret dropped a soft kiss on the top of her head.

"I tried asking him to stop," she said, fighting the feeling of nausea that rose at the memory. "But he kept on saying I'd enjoy it, kept saying Richard wouldn't mind."

Bret uttered a harsh expletive under his breath.

"I was so busy fighting him off, I didn't realize how loud I'd gotten until someone pushed open the kitchen door and everyone saw us." She did shudder then. "Richard went white."

"Probably from guilt," Bret said, his voice hard.

Nora looked up at him in the soft lamplight. "He was shocked. He told me so later."

"You don't think he had any idea that Benson had the hots for you?" Skepticism radiated from Bret.

"Of course not." She stared at him in puzzlement. It didn't make any sense that Richard would know and not warn her. After all, it had been his career on the line.

"Even if we give him the benefit of the doubt and assume that he didn't knowingly let his boss put the moves on you, Richard still comes out looking like a heel," declared Bret.

Nora didn't respond, startled at the thought.

Had Richard known of Benson's intentions? It seemed so incomprehensible. And yet, Richard had an uncanny insight into the weaknesses of his opponents. Wouldn't that naturally extend to his superiors as well?

The whole thing left her mind feeling muddled. "I should have handled it differently," she said with self-condemnation. "If I'd been more assertive, more determined, Mr. Benson would have gotten the message without everyone having to know."

"You're nuts," Bret said.

"I was so shocked I just started squawking."

Bret shook her gently. "You've got to get the blame pointed in the right direction. No woman should have to fight off a man in her own kitchen."

"But—"

"Think," he recommended. "Did you deserve to be attacked?"

"Of course not," she answered slowly.

"Did you deserve the crap that Richard handed you tonight?"

"No," Nora said definitely, fresh anger rising in her.

"Then let's put the blame where it belongs. Richard's a creep and you should have let me wipe the floor with him."

Nora shook her head. "I don't care about him. I just kept thinking about the riding school and how Mrs. Turner will never sell the land to me now."

"You don't know that," he said, stroking his hand down her arm. "Quit worrying about tomorrow and let's enjoy tonight."

His words hovered in the air, foreign and tempting at the same time. The shadowy cabin seemed warm and cozy as if it occupied a totally different world from the one they'd just left.

"When we were in high school, I used to watch you," Bret said. "You were quiet, but so cool and confident."

Nora's jaw dropped open. He'd watched *her* in high school?

"You were dating Richard, but every now and then," Bret went on, his voice soft and low, "I'd catch your eye and I'd wonder. . . ."

He bent to brush his lips against her cheek, a scatter of electricity along the point of contact jolting her.

With his arm around her, his hard, lean body pressed to hers, uncivilized urges hummed through Nora's blood. She sat on the couch in the quiet little cabin, surrounded by a sensation of comfort she'd never known. Not comfort in a soft, mothery sense, but a completion, a connection like a lock and key.

With Bret, she felt more of everything, as if the world suddenly shifted from gray monotone to technicolor.

Nora took in a deep, shaky breath. A white hot current seemed to run from his body to hers, replacing the fading anger at the humiliating scene she'd just endured.

"You've got a heart as big as Texas," he murmured. "But you've got to trust it more. Playing safe—it's only gotten you trouble. Trust your instincts, honey. Do what *you* want."

His words reverberated in her head. Do what she wanted?

A dangerous idea. What she wanted was him. She wanted his kisses, the taste of him on her tongue. Even the thought of that morning on the porch left her awash in a heady excitement.

She shouldn't have come here with him. The small space seemed too personal, so masculine. Nora battled with herself.

"What if I want . . . risky things?" she asked, her voice low.

"What's the point of living if you never take a chance? Haven't you ever been impulsive?"

A hundred sensual images spilled into her mind. *He* was everything she wanted.

Her breath caught in her throat. All her fantasies held him at the core. In them, she was a free woman, her forbidden desires no longer restrained. She wanted to seduce him to a mindless, desperate state. The thought had haunted her for days.

Nora went still when she realized she was actually considering it. Why not reach out to him? Why not finish the glorious episode they'd started on the porch that day?

Her teeth settled into the inside of her lip. She must be insane to consider it. But why not, she argued with herself. One night of passion didn't have to mean commitment. Never again would she trust herself to a man implicitly, but did that mean never knowing the exquisite pleasure of Bret's touch?

It would be a private moment between the two of them. And it didn't have to mean anything permanent. Bret wasn't the kind of man who wanted commitment.

Nora's heart thundered in her chest. Her body felt ablaze already, leap-frogging over any lingering hesitancy.

He reached up, brushing back a strand of hair from

her cheek. "Don't you ever want to do something wild and crazy?"

"Yes," she said shakily.

"Something just for you," he said, his voice low as he held her in the circle of his arms. She tilted her head back.

Quickly, she reached up for him, like a woman diving off a cliff. Her hand slid along the warmth of his neck, nestling there as she raised her mouth to his.

He felt so good, tasted so much like a hot August night, that she found herself kissing him like she'd always wanted to.

His mouth opened to her, meeting her with his own desire. Pressing closer, she deepened their kiss and felt the thunder of his heart revving like an engine.

"Nora?" His breath was ragged when he lifted his head.

She opened her eyes and met the question in his. Tumultuous emotion possessed her—need, connection, yearning. *Please don't make me explain!* Still, she supposed she had to say something. "I want you."

Tilting back her head, she slowly drew him down to her with agonizing slowness.

Bret held her in his arms, unable to resist her sweet, drugging kiss, but battling a conscience that nagged at him. What the heck was the woman doing kissing him like this?

He kissed her back, hungrily, his mind racing even as his body demanded more. The effort to keep himself in check made his muscles burn with bunched tension. Nora moaned, the glitter of her eyes visible as she pulled back a fraction. She drew her hand down the front of his shirt, finding and opening three buttons before Bret captured her with his own hand.

"Honey." His voice sounded strained to his own ears. "You've had a rough night. Maybe I'd better get you home." It was the noblest thing he'd ever said in his life.

"Don't you want me?" she breathed, nipping at the corner of his mouth. "I want you."

"Nora, for God's sake," Bret groaned. Every touch made him crazier. Just sitting beside her for the last half hour had been an act of sheer willpower.

She turned to face him more fully. "You told me to act on my impulses, to do what I want to do."

Jeez, he was an idiot. He'd encouraged her to act boldly and now his biggest fantasy had just become a nightmare. How could he make love to her when she'd regret it in the morning?

Wreathing both arms around his neck, she nuzzled his shirt collar. "This is what I want. And this." She pressed herself against him, her breasts soft and enticing.

He groaned again, bending swiftly to capture her mouth in a rough kiss, wrestling his own urges with limited success. This was the wild side of Nora, her hungry little mouth clinging to his as she pressed her body to him.

"You'll wake up tomorrow and hate me." *Go with it!* His body demanded. "God knows I want you so bad I've been walking funny for six weeks. But don't go to bed with me to spite the town."

"I could never hate you," she said, wriggling closer. "I've dreamed about making love with you. I haven't been able to sleep since the other day for thinking about the way you touched me."

Bret stared down at her, his indecision swiftly fading.

"Make love to me," she asked. "I know what I want."

He moved then, bending his head to capture her mouth, hot and hungry. "No regrets," Bret commanded between kisses.

"None," she promised breathlessly as she tore open the rest of his buttons and brushed her hands over his chest, cool and seductive.

Fumbling to get closer, he hauled her onto his lap, his hand cupping the curve of her breast. She arched to him, her breath coming in little pants. He stroked her through the thin cotton of her shirt, teasing her nipple. Nora moaned, her head falling back over his arm.

Once nestled on his lap, he held her closer still, his hand caressing her soft flesh as he sought her mouth. Need tore at him, fierce and hot, consuming any rational thought. She was here with him, wanting him, and he was swamped with an overwhelming drive to lose himself in her.

He had to get a grip. At this rate, he'd rush her and end up embarrassing himself. Nora bent to press her face against his chest, where his shirt was still open from her earlier foray. "Damn," he muttered, his arms tight around her.

Bracing his legs, Bret surged off the couch, carrying her toward the bedroom with large strides. The door slammed back against the wall as he carried her into the dark, cool room. He tilted her onto the bed, straightening to rip off his shirt. She knelt on the bed, her flushed face visible in the light filtering in from the living room. With her dark hair tumbled around her shoulders, she waited for him. He could see her trembling and recognized the desire in her eyes.

He closed the distance between them in a heartbeat, carrying her back against the flat surface of the bed.

How long had he hungered for her? Ached for her as he tossed in this very bed? Ever since she'd come home, she'd lingered in his mind, driving away thoughts of other women.

He joined her on the bed, kneeling beside her to cup her head in his hands and hold her still for his kiss. Long, slow kisses, one after another until he could feel the molten hush of his blood through his veins.

Moist and tender, her lips were sweeter than anything he'd ever tasted. He held her, his hands in her hair, her fragrance surrounding him. Her face seemed a pale blur in the twilight that filled the room. The contours of her eyes, nose and cheekbones formed a hazy beauty that he knew would haunt him forever.

Her hands rested on his arms, the slender fingers splayed on his bare flesh. He felt as if he were on fire and wondered that he didn't burn her where she touched him. A swift pulse fluttered in her throat where his thumb pressed. Bret bent to kiss her there, sliding his hands over her shoulders to find the row of small buttons on her shirt.

An almost expectant silence filled the room, only broken by their shuddered breathing and the hush of fabric leaving skin. He tugged at her shirt, drawing it open to reveal her skin. In sunlight, she took his breath away, but in the scattered light of this sheltered room, he felt as if his heart had been pierced by her beauty.

Taking advantage of his pause, Nora drew her hands across his shoulders, exploring his chest with eager fingers. She bent forward, pressing her lips against his bare skin, tasting him with quick flutters. Bret clutched the bed to keep from throwing her back and having his way with her.

As she trailed kisses along his shoulder, he worked at unhooking her bra. His years of practice in the activity might have been more helpful had he been less distracted.

As it was, he felt as unskilled as a sixteen-year-old boy heading for second base. Her hair floated forward, falling against his shoulder in a soft drift. He found himself overwhelmed with tenderness. He couldn't imagine a more precious moment. With Nora huddled in his arms, eagerly exploring his body, offering hers so enthusiastically, a sudden rush of emotion flooded him.

Holding her close, a sensation flickered inside him that he couldn't identify. He wanted to love her, to keep her safe from Richard and the gossips. He wanted to see her fly. She deserved so much more.

With her scent surrounding him, her eager hands caressing him, Bret hungered for all of Nora—her sweet welcoming body and her fierce, bright spirit, all wrapped around him.

Nora felt her bra come free in his hands. She shivered partly with the coolness of the room and partly from anticipation. His hands were warm on her back, his callused palms gliding over her as if she were the first woman he'd held.

He bent to her breast, his mouth damp and hungry. A spasm of sheer pleasure shot through her and she clutched at him for support. Nora squirmed with each stroke of his tongue. Craving, hot and fierce, sprang every nerve to attention. His touch set off sparks.

Bret straightened, leaving the bed to strip off his jeans. A shaft of light illuminated his nakedness, the lean line of his body, the muscled shape of his legs and buttocks. She itched to touch him everywhere, trace every enticing contour.

Fumbling with the snap of her own jeans, she

skimmed them off and waited, naked in the cool night air.

He joined her on the bed, his body warm against hers, the thrust of his arousal smooth and hard against her leg.

"You're so beautiful," he murmured, the stroke of his hand slow along the curve of her hip.

Her wayward hands couldn't stop touching him, the powerful slope of his back, his tight behind and strong thighs. In places, he felt smooth and warm like a rock in the sun; in other places, rough with body hair.

Touching Bret was like entering a foreign country where everything was new and magic.

Touch melted into touch. Nora pressed against the length of him, hard against soft, marveling at the glorious differences. She moaned as he fondled her breasts, stroking and molding her flesh until a deep, aching longing settled low in her body.

He leaned over to kiss her, deeply, hungrily, his hands stroking over her belly and thighs. Rising, he moved between her knees and paused, staring down at her. He trailed a hand down her inner thigh, his touch whisper soft, almost reverent.

Nora arched toward him, empty and yearning, her body calling out to his. He brushed a finger against her most sensitive spot, his movement agonizingly slow. The roar in her ears increased a notch, the blood pounded through her veins like flood tides.

She reached for him, urging him forward.

"Wait a sec, honey." His voice was strained as he got off the bed and rummaged in a drawer. "Damn." Slamming it shut, he pulled open another and heaved the contents onto the dresser.

Propped on an elbow, Nora watched his search with a concerned anticipation that turned to relief when he pulled a dark square from the pile. Returning to the bed, Bret tore open the packet and swore to himself, fumbling to put on the condom.

He slid between her legs, bending to kiss her again. Their tongues met as he slowly entered her body. Pleasure rippled through Nora. She bent her legs, her body welcoming him. Each movement brought a cascade of sensual bliss.

They rocked together, locked in each other's arms, lost in their own private paradise. She felt the roar and sweep of her blood, the raging, driving rush of her heart. He was everything. Ecstasy.

Taking him in, she stroked him with her body, cherished his rising excitement as they hurtled toward release, each pulse faster, each thrust harder. She felt rather than saw a sudden burst of light showering through every cell, and then a sensation of free fall as her body clenched around his.

Dimly, she heard his hoarse cry, felt the spasming of his body as he joined her in the heavens.

They drifted down together, clinging to one another with soft murmurings and touches.

Stars still seemed to spin above Nora when she opened her eyes in the darkness, marveling at a moment that she knew had changed her forever.

How could she have thought that making love to Bret just this once would satisfy her? And how was she ever going to keep her heart safe now?

Chapter Seven

Nora breathed in the warm, morning air as a mockingbird warbled from a nearby bush. Her riding helmet swung loosely from her fingers as she crossed the parking area in front of the barn.

The usual array of weathered vehicles there gave testimony to the size of Bret's ranching operation. Feeling strangely shy and excited at the same time, she noticed his truck parked near the barn and quickened her steps.

To her own amazement, she had no regrets about the night before, even though she'd gone home to sleep alone. She'd never been closer to heaven than during those moments in his arms.

As Nora entered the shade of the barn, a familiar high-pitched giggle made her steps falter. What was Cissy Burton doing here? Walking more slowly, Nora followed the sound of voices into the coolness of the barn, crossing to where the north door stood open. As she went, her ear recognized the lower tones mingled with Cissy's irritating voice.

Stopping in the open doorway, Nora saw them. Bret stood by the corral gate, screwdriver in hand as he tinkered with the gate catch. Standing close enough to breathe the same air was Cissy Burton, encased in tight jeans and a skimpy knit top.

"You're so handy," she said, giggling and smirking at him.

"Yes, ma'am," he winked as he continued his work. "I have all kinds of talents."

"I'm glad Daddy finally got around to cleaning his office. Bringing back that report he borrowed from you gives me a good excuse to visit, even if I do have to stop by four more ranches. He's terrible about borrowing things." She pouted prettily.

Bret straightened, grinning as he shut and opened the gate latch to check his work. "You won't mind running your dad's errands. It'll just give you a chance to flirt with all the ranch hands around here, you wicked heartbreaker."

Cissy giggled again. Bret's laughter joined hers, low and easy as he went on adjusting the gate.

Nora stood in the doorway, a sick feeling in the pit of her stomach. She'd known he was this way with women. Bret Maddock, the town risk-taker, horse race champion and heart slayer.

She'd always *known* he was a flirt. Every woman in town knew that. Last night hadn't meant anything special to him, it was clear. That fact should have comforted her. *She* was the one who had wanted to avoid complications.

But as she stood there watching him flirt with Cissy Burton, of all people, she wanted to throw up. Of course, his warm, flirtatious words meant nothing more than the bantering and sexual innuendo he shared with any willing, attractive woman.

He'd never promised her anything, never told her

he loved her, never said she meant more to him than a roll in the hay.

That was how she wanted it, she reminded herself furiously. So why did she want to hurt him at this moment? God, she'd let him get to her, let him come to mean something. She'd made the stupid mistake she'd sworn never to make again.

Nora took a step forward, and Bret's head turned toward her.

"Nora." His smile welcomed her and she found herself struggling with an overwhelming impulse to smash his teeth in.

Cissy glanced over, another smirk crossing her face. "That was some party you missed last night, Nora. Richard is a wonder on the dance floor," she finished with satisfaction.

Richard could have made love to Cissy on the floor of the VFW hall for all Nora cared. Not with her world splintering around her. Without saying a word, she turned away, blindly heading back into the barn.

"Nora," Bret called. "I didn't know you had lessons today."

She swiveled around automatically.

"I don't have any," she spoke for the first time, her voice feeling rusty in her throat. "I'm just taking Chessie out."

"Hang on a minute and I'll go with you," he offered. "This gate is almost finished."

Cissy glanced between the two of them, obviously unsure how to interpret the interchange.

"No, thanks," Nora said stiffly. "I'd rather ride alone." She spun on her heel and left the doorway.

"My! How rude." Cissy's voice followed her.

Bret said something to Cissy, his response too muffled to hear. Nora reached Chessie's stall and quickly saddled the mare.

Absorbed in her need to get away and try to make sense of the emotions jumbling in her, Nora barely noticed footsteps echoing in the barn, followed by the revving of an engine. After securing Chessie's girth, she took the reins to lead the horse out of the barn.

Bret stood in the opening. "Are you okay?"

"I'm fine," she said, glancing at him just long enough to register an uncertain expression on his face. A few more steps and she was outside, Chessie dancing beside her.

With trembling hands, she mounted the horse and urged her away from the barn. *Please don't come after me,* she prayed.

Almost unconsciously, she took the opposite direction from the way they'd ridden together. Her hurt was too fresh, her mind too confused to confront the sweet memories of that day, their passionate abandon on the porch of the Turner house.

All around her, the air was fresh with birdsong and humming honey bees. Nora rode on sightlessly, oblivious to everything.

What a fool she'd been. Was she doomed to be this way always? Unable to keep her heart safe? When would she stop handing her life over to other people, first to Richard and now—without even knowing it—to Bret.

Setting Chessie on a path, Nora wrestled with memories. Bret had been right about one thing. She'd never really loved Richard. At the time it hadn't seemed liberating, but the debacle with Benton had set her free. If it weren't for him, she might not have realized how unsatisfying her life was.

Sad to say, even with the gossip and hostility in Stoneburg, these past few months had been the best of her life. She was doing something she'd always wanted to do. And her student list was growing steadily, despite Cissy and Richard's mother.

True, Nora still faced the hurdle of convincing Mrs. Turner to sell her the land. In all likelihood, that dream had been dealt a death blow last night. With her illustrious background, Mrs. Turner had a reputation to maintain. Why would she sell her family's homestead to a woman who caused such controversy?

The greatest heartache was Bret, however. Nora had been fooling herself to think she could indulge her passion for him and not get burned. Like an idiot, she'd fallen in love.

Surely, he'd never meant to earn her heart. He was a captivating man, ever willing to engage a woman's attention, but he never courted entanglement.

Nora's chin lifted, her hands steady on Chessie's reins. Regardless of the mess she'd gotten her heart into, she had to take charge of the situation now. Working at the Maddock barn was no longer in her best interests. Seeing Bret every day and knowing he was spreading his charm around might just kill her.

If she wanted the Turner property, she'd have to go after it. She had planned on waiting until she was in a better position to ask for a loan. But she needed to take a positive step right now. The damage of last night's confrontation with Richard was done. Waiting another week or two wouldn't change what had happened, and she might as well make Mrs. Turner an offer today.

Shifting the reins, she turned Chessie back to the barn, determination giving her battered heart new hope. Trotting up to the barn, Nora noted with relief that Bret's attention was engaged with several men she didn't recognize.

She dismounted and swiftly walked Chessie past the group. Despite keeping her eyes focused in front of her, Nora felt Bret's glance on her, almost a physical touch as she passed. With swift, economical movements, she rubbed the horse down and watered her. Ready to go, she buried her face in Chessie's mane. "Wish me luck, girl. I'm going to seek our fortunes."

Chessie huffed, blowing softly against Nora's hand.

Leaving the stall, Nora walked around the front of the barn toward her car. If she could get there without having to face Bret, she'd be all right.

She'd have to talk to him eventually, but her feelings were too fresh to hide right now, and she'd probably burst into tears.

"Nora!" he called as she darted past.

"I can't talk now," she tossed back. Jumping into her car, she couldn't resist looking the rearview mirror as she backed out.

Wearing a perplexed frown, Bret watched her drive away.

Nora's steps echoed on the porch of Jim Carlyle's office. She'd discovered weeks ago from Hoyt that Carlyle handled Mrs. Turner's financial affairs. Finding his office had been a snap in a town as small as Stoneburg.

The wide, wrap-around porch of the converted house that served as Carlyle's office was empty save for the honey bees that buzzed in the bushes nearby. Nora pushed open the front door and found herself in a small parlor that appeared to be the reception area.

On the other side of the room, a door stood open revealing an inner office where a man sat bent over a desk. Nora felt her pulse skittering nervously.

Crossing the reception area, she paused by the

open door and knocked hesitantly. A chair squeaked as the man stood up.

"Come in," he invited her, his face open and friendly as he rounded his desk to usher her into the room. "I'm afraid my secretary is running an errand. Can I help you with something?"

"Are you Jim Carlyle?" Nora tried to keep her voice businesslike. He looked familiar, but she couldn't be sure if they'd gone to school together. The years changed people.

"I certainly am," he beamed as he offered her a chair across the desk. "Please sit down."

As he returned to his seat, Nora had a moment to study him. She'd been expecting someone different, more polished perhaps.

Jim Carlyle looked like a hundred other small town guys. A receding hairline topped his friendly face, and he wore a western-style plaid shirt beneath a corduroy blazer.

Nora felt her tension ease a little. The jumble on his desk held family photos, a smiling wife and kids. A dusty shelf behind his desk held a framed championship rodeo belt buckle.

She'd never seen one framed before, nor could she quite imagine him doing anything as adventurous as rodeoing. Still, his office seemed as open and above-board as he did.

"Now, how can I help you?"

Her heart rate picked up again. "I'm Nora Hampton," she said baldly, hating that she tensed for his reaction.

"Oh, uh . . . yes." Jim Carlyle cleared his throat. "How can I help you, Miss Hampton?"

"I understand you handle Mrs. Sara Turner's business affairs." Nora made herself meet his gaze calmly.

She was here to make him an offer, not to try to sell him a vacuum cleaner.

"Yes, I do." He looked puzzled, but still friendly.

Taking a breath, she forged forward. "Well, I'm interested in buying some property she owns—the old Turner homestead?"

"Umm, yes." Jim hesitated, clearly taken by surprise. "As far as I'm aware, that property hasn't been put on the market."

"I know that," Nora sat forward in her chair, "but I'm prepared to make Mrs. Turner a fair offer on the property, taking into consideration the condition of the land and buildings."

"Surely," he nodded. "Well, ah, I'll be happy to pass your offer along to Mrs. Turner if you bring me a formal contract."

Relief flooded her. He hadn't immediately dismissed her! She half expected him to bodily throw her from his office for her presumption. Standing up on shaky knees, she said, "Thank you. I'll have it back to you within a week."

"Certainly, certainly." Jim Carlyle rose with her.

Thirty seconds later, Nora bounded down the steps to her car, elated that she'd taken a significant step toward her goal.

She might have foolishly lost her heart to Bret in the last few weeks, but she could still salvage her dreams. Hopefully, focusing on the academy would ease her heartbreak.

"Please, please, Ms. Hampton. I'm just dying to learn how to jump," Kaybeth pleaded.

Nora considered the bright, youthful face looking up at her. "If you concentrate on your groundwork at our next lesson, we'll talk about jumping."

Kaybeth let out a whoop of joy.

"Remember what I said," Nora warned, as Kaybeth turned toward the barn, her hand on her horse's reins.

"I will," the girl promised, picking her way around a puddle of water left over from last night's rainstorm.

Nora's gaze followed the small figure as she headed toward the barn. Then she saw Bret, leaning on the corral fence, one boot propped on the crosspiece. His eyes met hers steadily.

A flush seemed to suffuse her body, the memory of tangled sheets and lovers' words flooding her mind.

The confrontation was unavoidable. They hadn't really spoken since the night at his cabin. Fortunately, she'd had some time to come to terms with her feelings.

She was an idiot. He was a typical irresponsible male, and she couldn't help loving him.

Stuffing her hands into the pockets of her jeans, she crossed the corral to where he stood. Caution told her to avoid him, cut off any interaction and bury herself in her work. But she knew that they would have to meet sometime.

"So am I still being punished for fraternizing with the enemy?" A faint smile hovered on his face, the tiniest hint of challenge in his eyes.

He had to mean Cissy. Nora shook her head.

"What were you mad about?"

"I'm not mad." She lifted her chin and decided to change the subject. "I went and talked to the guy that handles Mrs. Turner's business. I'm making a formal offer for the land."

Something unreadable flickered in his eyes and was gone. "So soon? You think that's a good idea?"

"Yes. I can't wait around for this town to forgive

me for something I didn't do," Nora declared with a snap.

A smile curled his mouth. "Attagirl," he approved.

Nora looked down, scuffing the toe of her boot in the damp ground as warmth flooded over her. His approval felt better than it should to a woman determined to regain her heart.

"Don't get too excited," she recommended. "I don't have her agreement to sell."

"Of course not, but it's a big step, taking on massive debt. Keep your eye on that bottom line," he encouraged, his eyes dancing.

She couldn't help but smile back at him, the insidious warmth he provoked melting her bones. Just his presence made the day seem more glorious, the air more invigorating.

"How about going for a ride?" he asked. "You owe me one."

"No, I don't," she retorted immediately.

"But you'll come with me, anyway?" he wheedled.

Hesitating, she looked away from his handsome countenance, battling her own urges with disgust. When would she learn?

"Okay," Nora agreed after a moment. She'd already lost her heart to him. How much more damage could one ride do?

Minutes later, she clutched the seat of Bret's banged-up jeep as they bounced over a cow pasture. "I had something different in mind when you mentioned riding," she called out over the roar of the engine.

Bret flashed her a grin. "This is just the beginning. You look like a woman who would enjoy a few loop-the-loops."

"What?" Nora grabbed at her seat as they jounced

over another rocky mound, her teeth nearly rattling in her head.

"You'll see," he promised with a wicked laugh.

They bounced over two more pastures, careening over the uneven surface at daredevil speed, the wind whipping Nora's hair into tangles.

Topping a rise, they coasted to a stop at yet another pasture, this one bare of cattle and flatter than the others. At one end of the field sat a small aircraft, its slender wings glinting in the sun.

Bret killed the Jeep's engine. "Welcome to my world."

Sweeping her hair out of her eyes, Nora surveyed the scene. "We're not really gonna do 'loop-the-loops,' are we?"

His laugh was low as he pulled her into a fierce hug. "I knew you were game."

Nora rocked back in her seat as he let her go, her senses still spinning from the rush of pleasure at being in his arms. "Wait a minute," she protested, realizing he was out of the Jeep and halfway over to the plane. "What exactly am I game for?"

Bret just kept walking.

Untangling her feet from a loose rope in the floor board, she got out and followed him across to the plane.

"I didn't know you had your own runway out here."

Bret snorted. "This is a pasture that works as a runway in certain seasons. I'll be moving the plane to an airfield soon. When the spring storms come, this place will be a pig wallow."

"But it's convenient most of the time," she observed, glancing around the pasture with its rippling blanket of green.

"Pretty convenient. It's too short for anything more than small aircraft." He hesitated. "I hope to build a real strip in the area. Something that can take bigger birds.''

"Sounds like a good idea.'' Nora couldn't help eyeing the small plane. Maybe she could wait and fly with him when he got that bigger plane.

"Isn't she a beauty?'' Bret touched the plane with pride.

"Umm, yes.'' Nora nodded and tried to look like she knew something about the subject. "Gorgeous.''

"And she flies like a dream.''

"I'm sure,'' Nora said, hoping she didn't disgrace herself by becoming hysterical if he actually did fly the plane upside down.

"Get in,'' he said. "I'm going to do a pre-flight check.''

"By all means,'' she recommended, skirting the tail of the plane as she went around to the passenger side. At least, she thought it was the passenger side. Were planes like cars?

Someone had thoughtfully designed a step on the wing, which gave her a clue on how to get into the thing. After wiping her boots, Nora scrambled up and climbed in.

The small cockpit looked like serious business, and she had to quell a rising panic at the thought of trusting her life to a heap of aluminum foil and Bret's luck.

Nora gnawed on her bottom lip, knowing she couldn't abandon ship now without disgracing herself, although she was sorely tempted to bail.

Fortunately, he climbed in before her anxieties got the better of her good intentions.

"Here, let me help you with the belt.'' He reached across her body, his closeness stirring a warmth in her.

Within seconds, she was strapped in, her heart

pounding too loudly in her chest. She tried to calm herself during Bret's preparations. He seemed completely relaxed, as if he were going to ride a bicycle.

Nora felt some of the tension seep from her. Somehow, she knew he wouldn't let her be hurt—physically, anyway.

In a few short moments, he flipped a switch and brought the airplane to life. The little craft shook with the spin of the propeller, the noise of the motor making Nora's ears ring.

She forced herself not to clutch the seat as the plane started forward, bouncing over the meadow. Each bounce seemed to take them higher until they lifted from the ground, airborne on a smooth stream of wind.

The earth fell away behind them as they climbed, and Nora peered out the window. A childlike feeling of wonder crept over her as she watched patch after patch of land drift beneath their wings.

The drone of the engine seemed more steady with just the slightest tremor every now and then. As her nervousness diminished, Nora felt herself relaxing into the movement of the small plane, allowing herself simply to be suspended. Overhead, the sun shone with a gentle springtime brightness.

The whole town lay beneath them, the structures and streets familiar and yet different than she'd ever seen them. From up here, it looked like a perfect town, peaceful and welcoming. The plane droned on like a huge bumblebee, carrying them away.

"Look down," Bret called to her over the noise. "The courthouse at Montague."

Glancing out the window, she spotted the ornate building, their overhead angle making it look like a wedding cake constructed of pink granite.

"I can see why you like it up here," she said, earning an encouraging smile from Bret.

"It's great, isn't it?" His face was a picture of confidence, so comfortable at the controls of the aircraft that he didn't appear to even think about it.

Maybe that was why he'd caught her heart unawares. That cocky self-possession of his drew her like a promise. Somehow he'd gotten around her defenses.

"Want to fly over to Lake Arrowhead?"

"Sounds good."

He tilted the wings, sending them arching to the left before settling the plane on its course. Time seemed suspended as they took an aerial tour of the northern boundary of Texas. Nora studied the instrument panel with its array of delicate gadgets. She found herself staring at Bret's hand resting on the throttle, her mind flooded with memories of their night together. She recalled the touch of his hand on her body.

She wanted to feel all those things with him again. Wanted to be held in his arms again. There was such intoxication in his kisses, such treacherous promises of ecstasy. Even though she knew she didn't have his love, each touch felt like heaven.

Stupid, stupid urges.

Tomorrow, she'd be good, she told herself. Tomorrow she'd worry about her betrayed heart. Today, she just wanted this golden time with him—no doubts intruding. One more opportunity to do what she wanted, no matter the consequences. Nothing was certain between them except her eventual grief, but she found herself aching for the part she was sure of. He wanted her. For now, for this moment, that was enough.

They glided low over Lake Arrowhead, watching

the glitter of the sun off its surface, broken only by a flicker of light that might have been a fish leaping up out of the water.

As they turned back to the ranch, Nora leaned her head against the seat, lost in a sense of abandon. The whole afternoon left her feeling both peaceful and exhilarated, alive and vibrant. A fine hum of tension seemed to flow through her veins, a flutter of excitement and anticipation.

She'd entrusted herself to Bret and only good had come of it, this time. He flew the plane like a consummate professional.

There weren't any good answers to handling the scandal. There was no way to take back her love for him, but she could lose herself in being with him, just for awhile.

Bret glanced over at Nora. She lay back against the seat, her body soft and relaxed, like a woman awaiting her lover. He felt his pulse rev at the thought, a fierce, possessive response that still puzzled him. From the moment she'd turned to him that night at the cabin, he could only think of her as his own.

He leveled off the Piper as they approached his makeshift airfield, and pulled back on the throttle. The plane drifted toward the earth, dropping down with a smoothness that never failed to gratify him. They skimmed over the ground, lower and lower until the landing gear just grazed the grassy surface, settling down with hardly a bump.

Even as he taxied down the runaway he couldn't help but congratulate himself on the difference in Nora's mood at take off and at landing. Gone was her white-knuckled grip on the seat and her expression of terrified, silent prayer. She sat quietly, watching him, the expression on her face making it difficult for him to concentrate.

He still couldn't figure what happened to her the other day. She'd seemed fine when he'd dropped her off at her mother's house after their incredible lovemaking. Even her insistence on going home that night had seemed reluctant.

It was maddening that he couldn't understand what was going on in her mind. For once, he was clueless as to a woman's feelings for him. And when had he begun giving so much thought to what was between them?

All he knew was that he wanted her, right now, always. And while her eyes told him that she wanted him, too, he found himself frustrated still by the thought of the Turner property.

What the heck was he going to do when she found out he'd bid on it, too? He hadn't thought she'd carry her riding school this far. And who knew whether anything would come of it still? There were a lot of hurdles to becoming a landowner, particularly when you had no credit record and a hostile business environment. Things might still work out smoothly; when Nora gave up the riding school idea, there'd be no barrier to their relationship. He just had to hang in there till it all played out.

Bringing the plane to a halt, Bret glanced at Nora. "I hope landing didn't shake you up," he said.

"Not at all," she said, smiling.

Pleased with her answer and enjoying the warmth of her smile, Bret got out and began securing the plane. Shoving the chocks into place, he reflected again how grateful he was that they had the wide open spaces to themselves. In the city, a clear day like today meant crowded skies and traffic on the runway.

Glancing over his shoulder, Bret saw Nora standing beneath an unusually large oak at the fence line. The warm spring afternoon hung over the meadow like a voiceless dream that heated the blood and roused every instinct.

He finished up the tail tie-down and closed the plane, fighting the urge to hurry. The quiet in the meadow was broken only by the buzz of insects and the occasional call of a bird. Even with the ranch so far from town, cars and tractors could be heard at the house. Out here, a complete isolation wrapped them together.

Bret walked over to where Nora stood, his whole body vibrating with hunger for her touch, her kiss.

"So . . . was it good for you?" he asked when she turned to face him. The humor in his question hid a real need to hear more of her reaction to flying with him.

"I liked it," she said slowly, her eyes focusing on his face. "A lot. I can see why you do it. It's like being set free, without even the earth to hold you."

Something warm and resonant loosened inside him. "Tell my father that. He's convinced I have a death wish."

Nora smiled, her expression empathetic. "Somehow I never pictured you has having an over-protective parent."

"There's lots you don't know about me," he growled, reaching out to draw her into his arms.

She came to him without resisting, her head thrown back to look into his face. Bret held her there, the soft brush of her hair teasing his arm.

"I want you so bad, I hurt," he murmured.

He felt the tremor go through her, a longing that surfaced in her eyes.

She hesitated only a second, her voice almost a whisper. "Shall we go to the cabin?"

Her willing acquiescence made the blood jump in

his veins. Bending, Bret kissed her, the play of their mouths and tongues stoking the fire in him. She felt small and soft in his arms, need and longing all wrapped in the sweetest, most fragrant package he'd ever held.

Chapter Eight

He drew her down to the ground, the thick grass beneath the tree cushioning them. Every kiss pulled them closer to the flame. Bret sampled her mouth over and over, his hands urgent on her body. Everything about her enflamed him, the sweet curve of her bottom in his hands, the catch of her breath when he nibbled beneath her ear. He felt her hands on him, urgent and restless.

The softness of her mouth beneath his was hungry and giving. He pulled her closer, seeking contact even through their clothing. She moaned when he cupped her breast in his palm. Bret unbuttoned her shirt swiftly, pulling back the fabric to find one nipple with his mouth. He stroked her, reveling in the feel of her skin against his.

He felt her writhing beneath him, her head thrown back, her legs intertwined with his as he rocked against her. Moving to suckle her other breast, Bret tried to slow the pace. He fondled her, his free hand sliding down to the apex of her thighs. Even through her jeans, he could feel the heat of her body. Slowly, he cupped her, his own excitement rising with her every moan.

Never in his life had the blood pounded so hard in his veins. He couldn't analyze it, didn't even want to think about it. Some things didn't need evaluation.

Later, he'd worry about the future, about her reaction to his offer on the land. Now, he wanted her more than anything, needed the moments in her arms like a drug.

"Bret," she gasped, "someone . . . might see."

The fog in his mind cleared enough to reassure her. "There's no one here." His voice sounded unnatural and rough to his own ears. "The ranch hands are in the east pasture."

His hands unerringly loosened her belt and the button at the waist of her jeans. He pulled her shirt free and his hand met the smooth glide of her stomach.

"You're sure there's . . . no one around?"

"Yes." He couldn't think, couldn't lose himself in her fast enough. Still, he struggled to stay in control. Nora murmured and moved eagerly against him, her lips reaching for his, her hands tearing at his clothes. He held still as she tugged the shirt from his back, enjoying the silken glide of her fingers.

Her lips traced a warm path along his collarbone, each kiss a declaration. Every movement—the press of her bare breasts against his chest, the stroke of her hands on his belly—told of a woman on fire. She kissed him with an open hunger, an unashamed sensuality that made him wild.

Kneeling, Bret drew her up with him. He skimmed her jeans down her slim hips. Poised on her knees beside him, her open shirt hung from her shoulders, her front-hook bra dangling like a miniature vest. He became more aroused as he looked at her. Her breasts were bared to his gaze, the nipples erect, the soft hair between her thighs luring him closer.

Snatching up his shirt, he threw it on the ground behind her and gently urged her back so he could wrest her boots from her feet. In seconds, her jeans landed in the grass, her slender legs apart in the most erotic pose he'd ever seen.

He shucked his own boots and jeans in record time. Kneeling in front of her, Bret bent to kiss her breast, then moved down to the delicious softness of her stomach. With one hand, he cradled the small of her back as he sought the soft, moist treasure between her thighs. He traced the softness, the damp flesh there an invitation. Her thighs were warm and firm against him.

He felt her shudder, the action sending a ripple through his own body as if they were connected. The faint trembling in his muscles signaled the slipping away of his control.

He'd never felt so joined with a woman, never needed anyone the way he needed Nora now. Her skin glowed in the light. Hunger and yearning thudded in his stomach like a fist, sucking the air out of his lungs.

He knelt before her, struggling to draw in his breath, a clog of emotion blocking his throat.

The sharp spring smell of new grass filled the air. Bret leaned toward her, stroking the full curve of her breast, loving the soft moan that escaped her as her head fell back.

She slid a hand over his shoulder, smoothing down over his chest to pause at his heart. Her knees widened ever so slightly as her hand dropped lower. Bret flinched as she found her goal. Exquisite shafts of sensation followed every movement of her hand. He steeled himself to hold still against the pleasure, to let the raging sensations ripple over him.

Her touch whispered over his heated arousal, light but not hesitant. She seemed to love the shape of him, the palm of her hand smoothing every sensitive inch.

Bret felt his teeth clench, heard a swishing of blood in his veins, and knew he had to draw back. He gripped her hand, stilling her movement as he bent his mouth to hers.

This time, he didn't fumble with the condom. Every movement was swift and sure, driven by passionate, consuming need. Kneeling before her, he entered her welcoming dampness. With every push there was a pull, a rocking, driving union that put his body in shock and displaced his mind. He felt locked with her, in her, blindly, completely given over to her. Every thrust felt like a further connection, a fusing of hearts and bodies. Setting her arms back over her head, he bent to kiss her breasts.

She tasted of heaven and earth and everything in between. Bret felt the sudden trembling of her body, heard her gasping breath as her body spasmed around his. She called out his name as if searching for a lost lover.

The rushing of his breath caught in his chest as he buried himself in her, driving toward the highest, brightest moment. In a spinning, racing tumble, he felt every part of himself splintering into ecstasy.

He might have called out her name as well. All he knew was the touch of her around him as he shuddered. Burying his head in Nora's neck, he drew in the sweet smell of her and, for the first time in his life, fought back a sudden moistness in his eyes.

Nothing had ever prepared him for loving Nora. He rolled onto his side, drawing her with him, locking her in his arms, unable to speak. For once, he could find no words.

Suddenly, everything was up for grabs and he knew he would fight whatever battles were required to keep her in his life.

"Dammit, Jim! I know she offered less for the land than I did. How much less?"

"Quite a bit," Jim said heavily, his face clouded.

"I could withdraw my bid," Bret said, his words coming slowly as he slouched in the chair across from his friend's desk.

"You've been after that property for years," Jim reminded him. "It's the best place for your airstrip. That Beechcraft Barron you've been looking at won't land in a cow pasture."

"I know." Bret's hand clenched. The downside to knowing how to finagle things in life was that you ended up wanting it all.

"Nora will get over losing the property. There are other places she can set up that riding school of hers."

"She has her heart set on this land," Bret said grimly.

"Maybe you could just talk to her," his friend suggested. "Tell her that you've had your eye on that plot since way before she came back to town. That having the airstrip right there—"

"I'm not in that good with her," Bret interrupted with an irony he knew Jim couldn't appreciate. Nora's hunger for him was as immediate and intense as his was for her, but she'd never given the least hint that she'd give up her dreams for him. And something inside him didn't want to ask her to.

Jim snorted. "You haven't met a woman you can't charm."

"My reputation is way overblown."

His friend laughed. "Excuse me? I remember the crowds of women around you when you were rodeoing. And you're a local hero after winning the Association race ten years in a row."

"There's only so much mileage you can get out of that."

"Get real," Jim protested. "You never have to buy your own beer. Every cowboy within twenty miles around dreams of breaking your streak."

Bret shook his head. "Maybe so, but that doesn't have anything to do with Nora."

"Of course it does. Women like winners."

If only things were so simple. Bret stared out the window behind Jim's desk, not really seeing the streaming rain. "Things with Nora— Well, I just don't want to blow this."

Surprise broke over Jim's face. "So you're just going to withdraw your offer? That doesn't seem reasonable from a business standpoint. Mrs. Turner might not even consider Nora's offer." He broke off, looking flustered. "It is low."

"And Nora is Stoneburg's official Jezebel," Bret inserted for him.

"Well, it's probably just mean spirited talk. Some folks don't have anything better to do." Jim shuffled some papers on his desk.

"They're talking, all right." Bret straightened from the chair. "You're right about one thing, Jim. I don't have to do anything right this minute."

It could still work out. There were at least a dozen obstacles to Nora getting that land. And even if she did manage to overcome them, things had gone too far for him to confess now.

Too many people knew about his plans for the Turner property. If he withdrew his bid, Nora could still hear about it. And if she did, he was likely to see an ugly end to her warm embraces. On some level, she still held back from him, even without knowing of his interest in the property she coveted.

Bret shoved his hands into his pockets. He'd just have to bide his time and hope his luck held out.

"Just come look at it, Nora," Bret said, propped against the stall as he watched her fussing with Chessie's tack. "There are fifteen acres just outside of Bluegrove. It has a barn that's in pretty good condition and plenty of room for a riding ring."

She brushed at a spot of mud on the leg of her jeans. "I can't now. I have to go change. I have that appointment with Mrs. Turner this afternoon."

"That's hours away. We'll run over to Bluegrove, see this property and be back with time to spare."

"You must think she'll reject my offer. That's why you want me to look at this other property," Nora accused.

Bret tried to draw her into his arms. "It never hurts to have options. Maybe you'll like this place better."

"I won't." Nora tugged free, remembering her promise to herself to try and stay Bret-free for at least a day. Ever since they'd made love in the pasture, she'd felt irrevocably bonded to him, connected in a way that made no sense. Despite all she knew about men, everything felt different with him.

Even though she knew it wasn't.

It still amazed Nora that she'd allowed herself to roll around naked in an open field with Bret. There'd still been no talk of love between them. If she'd completely left sanity behind, she'd ask him how he felt about her. But the thought of an answer she didn't want to hear left her paralyzed.

Still, she loved him, even without knowing the terms of their relationship from his viewpoint. With her heart wide open, she was taking the biggest risk of her life.

"Do you think anyone would notice if we got naked right here and did the wild thing?" Bret murmured against her temple as he cupped her bottom. "I've taken to carrying a few condoms."

Nora squirmed in his grasp, her body heating to near readiness at the thought. "We're in the middle of a busy barn," she said shakily as he nibbled her neck. "Anyone could walk in."

"Let's risk it. All I can think about is making love with you." He caressed her breast through the chambray shirt she was wearing.

"Bret, please," she whispered raggedly. "One of your ranch hands could walk in."

"Okay." He straightened with a regretful sigh. "At least come with me to this property. It's a glorious day. We should enjoy it since we're bound to get another thunderstorm soon."

"I don't know," she hesitated, struggling with an urge to go home and get dressed for the appointment.

"Come on. It'll take your mind off Mrs. Turner." He took her hand and tugged gently, leading her out of the stall.

"Are you sure we'll be back in time for me to change? I can't go to see Mrs. Turner smelling like a horse."

"We'll just nip over there and come right back. I promise." He tucked her hand in his. "And I try never to break a promise."

"You have to do more than try," Nora threatened, allowing the distraction of his presence to lift her anxieties. There was too much riding on the meeting this afternoon.

She followed him to his Jeep.

All around them, birds chattered, saturating the warm air with the sounds of spring. As Bret started the Jeep, Nora stretched her arms up, filling her lungs with the scent of grass.

A foolish sense of contentment flooded her as they drove out of the barnyard. It was the same sensation she'd carried with her since making love with Bret under the tree. Only her anxiety about getting the land ruffled her bizarre sense of well-being.

Her life had never been more disrupted or uncertain. She lived under her mother's roof, unable to afford a place of her own, the people of Stoneburg were still convinced she was a hussy, and she'd lost her heart to a man who would only hurt her.

She lifted her face to the rushing wind. So why she did she feel so thrilled just to be alive?

As they jounced down the dirt road, rutted by rains, Nora turned to study Bret, trying to temper the idiocy he caused in her. She'd been burned by a man before. What made her feel any more safe this time around? Her reverie ended as the Jeep bounced over a rut in the road, the movement lifting her out of her seat.

Bret pulled the vehicle to a stop where the gravel drive met the blacktopped road.

"How do you know about this place?" she asked.

He shrugged. "I drive over that way sometimes. I know a couple of people who live in Bluegrove."

"I saw you out riding General this morning," Nora volunteered, shoving back her windblown hair as he turned the Jeep away from Stoneburg.

"Yeah. Just getting a little work out."

"You looked good. I can see why the two of you have won the Association race so many times.

Bret grinned. "I'm not a bad rider, but General's the fastest horse in six counties."

"Chessie's pretty good too," Nora said with pride. "I bet we could give you a run for your money."

He glanced over, surprise on his face. "You think so?"

"Don't be misled by Chessie's manners," Nora warned him. "She has a great heart."

"I'm sure she has," Bret laughed. "But it'll take more than that to catch General."

Nora made a face at him. "You're so cocky."

"Maybe so." He threw an arm around her shoulder, the other hand carelessly controlling the Jeep. "I tell you what. Let's have our own personal race. And the winner gets to have his or her wicked way with the loser."

"You might be surprised," she warned.

"Possibly," he said, grinning at her.

Nora looked away. He obviously didn't believe she and Chessie were any competition. Leaning back against the seat, she let the subject drop. The day was too perfect to argue.

They sped along the quiet country roads, the occasional pickup truck pulling courteously onto the shoulder to allow them to pass. Farm-to-market roads webbed the countryside, a tangle of turns leading from Stoneburg to Bluegrove in the next county.

Nora leaned her head back against Bret's arm, soaking in the warmth of the moment and refusing to allow herself to worry about the meeting later this afternoon. The sun streamed down with a faint sizzle as it hovered near the pitch of the arching blue sky. The whip of the wind felt good against Nora's skin as they neared Bluegrove.

"The piece of land we're looking at is just west of town," Bret said as he turned the truck again.

"This is quite a way from where I am now," Nora

reminded him. "Most of my riding students are east of 287."

"That's the nice thing about Texas. People are used to driving with all this wide open space."

Within a few minutes, Bret turned off the highway onto a dirt road with deep, water-filled ruts.

The barn was visible from the road. A ramshackle gray structure with boards missing, it didn't look like a bargain.

She held her tongue as they jolted down the short, obviously unused drive. Although there were two other small buildings next to the barn, Nora couldn't see a house anywhere nearby.

Bret pulled the Jeep up in front of the barn. "Well, this is it." He got out and walked around to her side, holding out his hand. "Let's go in. I don't think they keep it locked."

"I wonder why," Nora said under her breath as he towed her toward the structure.

"I know it doesn't look like much now," Bret conceded as he dragged the barn door open. "But there's potential here and even the Turner property needs a lot of work."

"True. But not nearly as much as this place does." Nora peered through the dim light at several inadequate stalls.

"But you could probably get this place cheaper," he argued. "And you'd have more money for repairs. Let's look it over."

Nora followed him, picking her way around the debris that littered the wooden floor. Sunlight streamed through holes in the roof, the dusty shafts filtering down to illuminate a huge, splendid spiderweb.

Drawing in a sharp breath, Nora stepped back. "I . . . think I've seen enough," she groped her way gingerly back toward the door. Stepping out into the sunlight, she breathed a sigh of relief.

Bret followed her, pausing to shoulder the barn door shut. "Okay. There'd be a lot of clean up."

"Clean up?" she echoed incredulously, glancing back. "This place needs a wrecking crew. Or a strong wind."

"You're being negative," Bret chided. "Come around back. There's a great place for a riding ring."

Nora followed him, grateful for her jeans as she clambered over grass and weeds that reached up to her knees. The area behind the barn was level and open, not counting the weeds.

"Well?"

"It's a nice clearing," she admitted. "But in and of itself . . . I mean, it would have to be mowed and plowed, a fence put in. . . ."

"You'll have to do some of that with the Turner place, too."

"You're giving me such a hard sell, I have to believe you're sure Mrs. Turner is going to reject my offer," Nora said dryly, as he lead her around the barn to where the Jeep waited.

"Not necessarily," he said. "I think you're relying too much on getting that particular land. It never hurts to look."

"I've looked," Nora said, bending to scratch her ankle above her short hiking boots. "Can we go now?"

"I just want to show you one more thing." He climbed back into the Jeep. "Come on. We'll drive down to it."

Nora got in and hung on as Bret veered off the waterlogged drive and headed the Jeep over a field alongside the road. They jounced over the soft surface, the Jeep engine straining and whining as the wheels slipped.

"Exactly what are you showing me?" she shouted over the noise of the engine.

"A creek. It runs right through this place."

The Jeep slipped to the right and hung for a moment, its wheels spinning before catching harder ground.

"Maybe we should go back," Nora said, spotting bigger puddles as the ground sloped to the valley where the creek ran.

"We're almost to the road," he said. "There's a bridge I want you to see."

Hanging onto the windshield with one hand and her seat with another, Nora waited until the Jeep had come to a stop at a flat place not far from the creek. Trees grew thickly around the creek bed, their roots gravitating to the source of water.

Water rushed and bubbled over rocks, the shallow banks almost overflowing from the recent rains. To their right was the main route to Bluegrove, spanning the little stream by means of a picturesque stone bridge.

With the Jeep engine turned off, the only sounds to be heard were a delightful mixture of gurgling water and the song of birds. A damp carpet of new grass spread underfoot and the bright hue of tiny leaves sprang out from the branches overhead.

Nora glanced at her watch. A little over an hour until her appointment. "It's really beautiful, but why didn't we just drive down the road?" She gestured at the blacktop not eight feet away.

Bret grinned. "We get a better angle this way."

"Maybe so," she conceded, staring at the brown stains gathering around their footsteps, "but the ground is really wet."

"Just a little surface mud. Hey," he whispered suddenly, "we could go skinnydipping!"

Nora shifted out of reach. "We'd freeze."

"You wanted to take a bath before you see Mrs. Turner." He stretched out a hand as she backed away, laughing.

"No playing around. You promised to get me back on time."

He sighed heavily. "So I did. Okay, but I think we're missing a terrific opportunity."

Nora thought so too, but she didn't dare agree. Before she knew it, Bret would have her flat on her back, naked as the day she was born, locked in an ecstasy she had to give up.

Climbing back into the Jeep, she waited while he came around to join her. The engine roared to life and they rolled forward an inch or two when he pushed the clutch down. Nora grabbed at her seat again preparing for another rackety ride.

Shifting into first, Bret gave the Jeep some gas. The tires slipped on the grass and mud, the rear end sliding to the right.

Nora looked down in alarm, spotting a slick muddy patch under the wheel nearest her.

"Oh, no." She pivoted to face Bret.

"Relax." He stepped on the gas pedal again, trying to rock the Jeep out of the growing rut.

"I have to make this appointment."

"I know." He frowned. "Just hang on."

Minutes ticked past as he wrestled with the gas and the steering wheel, trying first one direction and then another.

"Here," he thrust the Jeep in neutral, "you give it the gas while I push." Jumping out, he went around to the back.

Nora nervously clambered into the driver's seat,

reluctant to drive the beast and unsure how to do what he wanted.

"You do know how to drive a stick shift, don't you?"

"Yes," she said. "But I've never driven a Jeep."

"Same basic principle," he said. "Just go forward."

"Well, I'm not going backwards when you're standing there," she snapped.

"That's a relief," he said, laughing.

"Can we just get going?"

"Sure. One-two-three, go."

Nora stomped on the accelerator. The engine bucked under her, whining and roaring, shaking the Jeep, but not moving.

"Wait a minute! Wait a minute!"

She swiveled around to look and, despite her growing anxiety, she had to bite her lip to keep from laughing. Bret was covered in mud from head to toe.

"Oh. Oops." She tried to keep the smile off her face.

"Yeah, oops." He wiped a glob of mud from his cheek and slung it away. "Just give it gas gently this time."

"Okay." Nora glanced at her watch again, and groaned. The minutes were ticking away. They just *had* to get out of here.

"Now," Bret called out. "Gently."

She pressed down on the gas pedal, concentrating to keep herself from losing patience with the stupid vehicle. Weren't Jeeps supposed to be able to go anywhere?

"Okay, okay," he yelled out again. "This isn't working." He slogged around from behind the Jeep looking like he'd been dipped in chocolate.

Nora didn't even smile, her anxiety over the appointment keeping humor at bay. "What now?"

"Now I try something different." He bent down

and rummaged under the driver's seat. "Have you seen a rope or a chain in here? I usually keep one under this seat."

"No." She ducked down, eagerly helping him look. "How are we going to use a chain?"

"There's a winch on the front of the Jeep," he pointed out, reaching back to explore behind the seat. "If we have a chain, we can hook it around a sapling and pull the Jeep out."

Nora glanced in the direction he gestured, noticing for the first time that when the rear wheels slipped toward the road, the front end pivoted toward a grove of small trees.

"But I'm not finding the damn chain."

The frustration in his voice comforted her some. At least he was taking this seriously.

Bret straightened and went around to the passenger side. "Where the hell is that chain? There's nothing in here. No chain, no rope." He searched a few minutes longer before standing up and staring into space as if scrutinizing his mind for the answer.

"Surely there's something in here," Nora bent to look under the seat, panic rising in her. After a moment she gave up, a helpless, doomed despair starting to creep in. She had to make that appointment with Mrs. Turner, and that was that.

"Let me try something else." He grabbed up some branches lying under the trees and pushed them down under the rear tires. Then he came around and got into the driver's seat.

For what seemed like hours, he coaxed the Jeep forward incrementally, again and again. Each time, it slipped back. Nora felt her nerves tightening and made herself promise not to burst into tears. They were losing precious time. There was no way she'd be able to get home, get dressed and make the appointment.

"If I could just get it to stay forward," he muttered, the Jeep idling between onslaughts. "What could we use as a rope?"

Nora didn't respond, using all her energy to keep from looking at her watch again and trying not to cry.

Bret glanced around the Jeep, his eyes stopping on a huddle of fabric in the rear. He laughed out loud, startling her.

"What's so funny?" she asked with an edge.

"Me," he chuckled. "How about we take off our jeans and use them with this denim jacket to make a rope?"

Swiveling around to gape at him, Nora wondered if he'd lost his mind. "A rope out of jeans?"

"You know, like using bedsheets to escape from a window," he laughed again.

"I'm glad you're finding this amusing," she muttered.

Bret stared at the windshield for a moment. "You know, it's not a bad idea."

"Are you nuts? You seriously think we could use our clothes to get this stupid thing moving?" Her voice rose with her frustration.

"Yeah, I do." He smiled at her, his eyes alight. "Come on, sweetheart. Get naked with me."

Chapter Nine

"I don't appreciate your joking at a time like this." Her voice trembled with the effort to remain calm.

"I'm not joking. I think this could work."

"How? How could it work?" she challenged him.

"We tie the jeans and the jacket together and knot them to that sapling," he nodded toward a nearby tree, "then we attach the other end to the winch and I crank us forward a little."

He looked at the distance between the tree and the front of the Jeep. "I don't think the jeans are strong enough to pull us out, but they might hold to pull us forward enough for the tires to catch solid ground when I give it gas."

Nora found herself envisioning the solution he mapped out. "Oh, this is ridiculous," she exclaimed. "We're out here in public and you want us to strip to our underwear?"

Bret glanced at the road. "There hasn't been anyone along since we got here nearly an hour ago."

"Still, it's crazy," she protested weakly, tantalized

by the possibility of salvaging her chance with Mrs. Turner. Showing up muddy and bedraggled would be better than not showing up at all.

Bret leaned forward, a teasing grin on his face. "Come on, Nora. It's not like we haven't gotten naked outdoors before."

Nora flushed at the memory conjured up by his words.

"You know you'll miss the appointment with Mrs. Turner if we don't do something fast," he said. "And unless you've got a better plan, we're stuck with mine."

She looked at him, indecision gripping her.

"You'll only have yourself to blame if you don't take this risk," he said, his voice soft. "Is the land worth it to you?"

"Yes," she said slowly. "It's worth it."

"Okay," Bret said, jumping out of the Jeep and beginning to loosen his belt. "Gimme those jeans, woman."

She climbed out of the Jeep, keeping the vehicle between her and the road as she shucked out of her pants. It felt strange to undress outdoors. The last time, she'd been wrapped in a passionate haze. Now she felt awkward and silly, wearing only a thin T-shirt, panties and hiking boots.

Her only consolation was that Bret looked just as funny, only slightly less exposed with his shirt tails covering his white briefs. Nora had to smile at the sight of his muscular legs disappearing into his muddy cowboy boots.

"Bring those here," he directed, knotting his jeans to the short chain attached to the winch. "We'll tie yours to mine and tie the jacket to the tree."

"You're sure this is going to work?"

"No." His strong hands tugged at the stiff denim.

"But it beats walking three miles to the nearest phone."

She watched him patch together the makeshift rope, pulling each knot taut and then looping one end around the sapling.

"Okay, I'm going to crank it forward and lock the winch. Then I'll start her up while you get behind and push."

"I have to push?"

"Which one of us is more likely to be able to drive this sucker out?" he challenged.

"I'll push."

"Good." Bret turned the crank on the winch slowly, pulling the denim rope taut. As he tightened it, she heard the popping of stitches but, amazingly, the makeshift rope held. Another half turn and Nora felt the Jeep ease forward a fraction.

"It's moving."

"Yeah," Bret acknowledged, his voice strained as he wrestled with the crank. "We need it a little further."

Two more turns pulled the vehicle incrementally forward before the rope emitted an ominous ripping noise.

"It's tearing!"

He stopped, getting into the Jeep. "Pray it's far enough."

He started the engine. Nora braced her arms against the back of the Jeep and planted her feet, preparing to shove. She heard Bret put the Jeep in gear and press the accelerator. The engine roared, and the wheels in front of Nora sent up a fine, wet spray of mud that covered her legs and chest. Ignoring the muck, she shoved against the Jeep, straining every muscle.

The wheels spun faster with the powerful whine of

the engine, mud splattering her legs and oozing down into her boots. Then she felt it, a movement forward, the smallest shudder, then a hesitation. Bret must have felt it too, because the engine suddenly revved faster until, in a lunge, the Jeep was free.

"We did it!" Nora straightened as he pulled the vehicle on to firmer ground, the roar of the engine ringing in her ears.

Caught up in the triumph of the moment, she stood looking at the Jeep, now on solid ground.

Bret turned around to grin at her. "I'll be expecting some pretty heavy gratitude."

"It's your fault we got stuck in the first place," she declared, wading through the mud puddle dug by the Jeep's tires.

"You know," he said with a smirk, "these muddy pastures are tricky. We could get stuck again while we're trying to get out of here. I'll drive more carefully if I have an incentive."

"I'll give you incentive!" She scooped up a handful of mud.

Bret started laughing. "You wouldn't."

Without hesitation, she let it fly, the loose, wet mud splattering just the side of his shirt as he moved to dodge her missile.

"That does it." He advanced toward her, as menacing as possible for a man wearing underwear and cowboy boots.

Nora turned and slogged away from him. "I don't have time for this," she shrieked. "Bret!"

"You started it." He grabbed Nora and caught her off balance.

She teetered for a moment before falling *splat!* on her rear. In a flash, Bret was beside her, his body shaking with laughter as he knelt and scooped her into his arms. "You make such a beautiful piggie in a mud puddle," he teased softly as his mouth came down on hers.

Passion exploded inside of her, mingled with relief. She clung to him, lost in the moment, knowing she should be getting up and hurrying back to town, but not caring. It had been so long since they'd kissed. He kissed her, his mouth magic on hers. Desire pounded through Nora, leaving her head buzzing. She found herself gasping as Bret lifted his head, looking at her with hunger in his eyes.

It was only then that the sound of an approaching engine broke through to her consciousness.

Nora whipped her head around, knowing in the flash of an instant that her worst fear was being realized. Here she was wallowing in the mud with Bret, half naked beside a public road. Her T-shirt and panties were plastered against her body, making her look like a refugee from a mud-wrestling match.

Stunned, she just stared at the car. The big old convertible sat only yards away.

In it was Cissy Burton with her parents. Three pairs of eyes fastened on them as the car rolled to a stop.

Her brain too numb to react, Nora had only her instinct to save her. Without hesitation, she rolled away from Bret and struggled to her feet before diving for the nearest bush. She hit the ground with a thud. Huddled behind the bush, she peered through the leaves trying to find Bret. *Please, God. Don't let them recognize us.*

Sometimes prayers weren't answered. From behind the bush, Nora saw Cissy's smile widen. Bret stood in the muck, his mud-splattered shirt tails flapping.

"I must say, Bret," Mrs. Burton's outraged voice carried clearly. "It's bad enough that young woman caused so much trouble for Richard. But here you are cavorting out in the open with her. You should be ashamed."

"We got stuck," Bret said, a smile hovering at the corner of his mouth. "We just got the Jeep out."

"Yes, and how unfortunate you were unclothed at the time," Mrs. Burton retorted to the accompaniment of Cissy's giggle.

Cissy's father cleared his throat, his amusement visible through the leaves of Nora's shelter. "I must say, that Nora Hampton does seem to enjoy getting a man's blood pressure up."

Nora felt her own blood begin to boil.

"So, uh. You need any help?" Sam Burton asked, grinning.

"No," Bret said, less amused. "No need to keep you folks."

Cissy trilled another giggle. "Oh, Bret. We're just going to see Aunt Sallie. You remember, you told me to say hi to her when I told you we were coming out this way today."

Nora gasped. *Bret knew the Burtons were coming this way today?* He'd known it and still suggested they strip?

"Hey, Bret," Sam called out. "I hear you finally made an offer on the Turner property."

Nora saw Bret's back stiffen, his body seeming to freeze.

Bret had offered to buy the Turner property?

"Uh . . . yeah. Well, thanks for stopping. We're fine."

"If that Nora thinks Sara Turner would sell her land to a hussy, she doesn't know anything." Mrs. Burton's voice rang triumphant. "Stoneburg isn't the place for that girl, after the scandal she caused."

A buzzing filled Nora's ears as she watched Bret

step closer to the Burton's car, his words an indistinct blur.

He was trying to buy her property.

She huddled in the bush, barely aware of the Burtons driving away, her mind a furious jumble of realizations.

He'd never mentioned his interest in the land. Why not?

All this time while he'd been encouraging her to take off her clothes and cavort with him—all along he'd wanted her land.

Bret had set her up. A dozen little things fell into place. Rage thundered through her. She'd given her heart to him and all he'd done was betray her.

"They're gone, Nora. You can come out."

Without his encouragement she'd have never gone to the Roadhouse, never shown up at the Association barbecue and had that public argument with Richard. Without Bret's pushing to come see this land today, she'd be sitting at Mrs. Turner's now.

Nora erupted from the bush. "You lying, cheating jerk!"

"Now, Nora." Bret held out a calming hand. "You don't have the whole picture."

"I thought I'd been set up before, but Richard can't touch you when it comes to deception." She stomped toward him, her feet sloshing in her mud-soaked boots.

"If you'll give me a chance, I'll explain," he said, his voice frustrated.

"You must want that land pretty bad," she said scathingly.

"I have had my eye on it for a while," he admitted. "It's the perfect place for my landing strip. But—"

"So you just set me up and watched me scheme and struggle to have my academy on that land while you made sure I never got it!"

"What are you talking about?" His face darkened with anger.

"All this time," she said, her voice shaking with betrayal and hurt, "you've been trying to get into my pants while plotting to keep me from getting the land!"

"What?" he said, his face conveniently thunderstruck.

"I've lost my one chance at the Turner property because you deliberately brought me out here today, deliberately got us stuck. Got me to strip off my clothes and stand naked by the road when you knew Cissy Burton would be coming by!" she shouted.

"That's not true!"

"I want to show you the bridge, Nora," she mimicked. "Go ahead, take off your jeans."

His eyes shifted, his expression darkening. "It's not the way it looks."

"No? So you haven't been after my land all this time? Haven't been deceiving me about that?"

"I never said I didn't want the Turner property," he said. "I just didn't talk to you about it—"

"You just snuck behind my back to make sure Mrs. Turner won't ever sell to me! This whole mess today! Look at me!" She gestured toward herself bitterly, the muddy T-shirt faithfully outlining every curve. "How long do you think it'll take the Burton family to spread the word about this little fiasco? Nora Hampton wallowing in the mud with Stoneburg's gift to womankind."

Bret took a step toward her. He paused, seeming to struggle with his words. "Nora, none of that is true. I did want the land, but not if it meant losing you. I love you."

"Bull!"

* * *

Somewhat later, Bret turned the Jeep down the tree-lined street to the small house, pulling into the driveway.

A movement at the front window of the neighbor's house across the street left Nora little doubt that they'd been seen. The old biddy who lived there knew Mrs. Burton well. She would have been one of first people alerted to Nora's latest crime. The news was probably all over town by now. Mrs. Turner would have long since heard the story behind her missed appointment.

Nora got out of the Jeep without a backwards glance. She'd given men the benefit of the doubt one too many times. Walking away was the only thing to do now.

She marched up the walk to the porch, determined not to scurry, not to give in to shame. Opening the door, she went in.

Let the town go into a feeding frenzy of gossip. She couldn't find it in herself to care anymore.

"Nora Hampton! Look at you!" Her mother appeared in the hallway. "I couldn't believe my ears when Madeline called. You must be out of your mind, rolling naked in the mud with Bret!"

Yes, she'd been out of her mind. And for a while there, it had been heaven.

"Couldn't you at least put your clothes back on?" Her mother followed her down the hallway.

"Mother!" The word came out forcefully. "I'm filthy, I'm tired and I don't want to discuss this subject right now."

"You may not want to discuss it, young lady, but—"

Nora went into her bedroom and shut the door,

ignoring her mother's startled gasp. Later, when she could be calm, she'd sooth her mother's worries. Now she had her own wound to tend.

Stripping off her muddy clothes in the adjoining bathroom, she stepped into the shower and turned on the water. A hundred thoughts beat against her brain as steam filled the tub enclosure. *She loved Bret Maddock*. No matter what he'd done, no matter what a snake he was—she still loved him.

But she couldn't let herself stay here and be worn down by his presence. Maybe he wouldn't keep pursuing her, but that was too big a chance to take. She'd have no self-respect if she let herself be seduced back into his arms after this betrayal.

The whole town must be laughing at how easily he'd stolen the Turner property away from her. She knew from living with Richard that men laughed about things like that.

When the worst of the mud was off, Nora cleaned out the tub and filled it, pouring in bubble bath like a medicinal tonic. She sunk into the hot, foamy water, submerging to her chin.

How long could a person hide in the bathtub?

Sighing, Nora sunk lower under the bubbles. She felt too battered by the events of the day to think coherently. She knew it was past time she stopped trying to ignore the talk. Before she left for good, she had a few things to say to several of Stoneburg's prominent citizens. But right now, she needed to get out of the bathroom.

Sloshing out of the water, she toweled off briskly and tugged on her robe. Much to her relief, her bedroom was empty when she opened the door. She'd half expected to see her mother there, waiting for an explanation.

Dressing carelessly in an oversized shirt and leggings, Nora began combing out her wet hair. Then, the doorbell rang.

She frowned, not recognizing the voice in the hall-way when her mother opened the door. Snatches of unidentifiable conversation drifted through the half-opened bedroom doorway.

"She's right in here." Sharon Hampton's voice drew closer. "Nora, you have a visitor," she announced, looking rattled as she ushered an immaculate Sara Turner into the bedroom.

Nora stared at the older woman, unable to believe her eyes.

"Good afternoon," Mrs. Turner said, her smile polite, her classic suit and pumps both beautiful and dignified.

Her greeting galvanized Nora forward, breaking the paralysis that kept her standing in front of the dresser, her hair brush clutched in her hand. "Mrs. Turner, I'm so sorry for missing my appointment with you this afternoon. I know it was terribly rude—"

The older woman waved her words aside. "That's quite all right. I understand you had a mishap."

Nora swallowed the lump in her throat, not knowing if she should go into the sordid details of the story. She glanced around the room, becoming conscious of the awkwardness of entertaining a visitor in one's bedroom.

"Won't you please sit down?" Nora gestured to a small armchair by the window.

"Thank you." Mrs. Turner sat down gracefully. Despite her years, she maintained a cool, composed social presence that left Nora conscious of her wet hair and bare feet.

Nora stared into the woman's face, overcome by an insane desire to take one more shot at buying the property, to finish what she'd started. Maybe there was still a chance she could get the Turner land. Rubbing Bret's face in it would be far more satisfying than running away.

"Mrs. Turner, about the offer I made on your homestead—"

Sara Turner crossed her legs and said serenely, "I'm sorry, my dear, but I'm not really prepared to discuss the property. There are many things to consider before accepting or rejecting any offer on that land."

"You're not prepared to talk about it?" Nora echoed with surprise. "But what about our meeting . . . ?"

"Yes, of course." An expression of self-consciousness flashed briefly across the older woman's face. "Actually, I've been wishing to talk to you for some time. The incident today compelled me to come here unannounced."

"The incident today?" Nora said hollowly.

"Yes." She paused, fidgeting with the handle of her purse. "I'm not sure if you know it, but I am not only the mother of a politician, but the daughter of one as well."

"Of course," Nora stammered, not sure where the woman was headed. "Yes, I do know that."

Everyone in town knew about her father, the illustrious Senator. It was a fact that often came up whenever the Senator's mayoral grandson came up for reelection.

"Then perhaps you will understand how I might sympathize with your difficulties lately."

Nora couldn't restrain her shocked, "You do?"

Mrs. Turner smiled briefly. "Why, yes." She stared down for a moment, seeming unsure how to continue. "It's easy for a young woman in the public eye to find herself in the position of having committed certain indiscretions."

Sara Turner cleared her throat quietly.

Sitting on the corner of her bed, Nora grappled with the image of a much-younger, indiscreet Mrs. Turner. "Yes, of course," she murmured.

"When I was a girl, a number of men paid me flattering attention." Mrs. Turner smoothed the fabric of her skirt. "I was usually quite circumspect. My mother held very strict views. But one man in particular . . . well, I thought I was in love with him. He was older, you see, and very charming. I didn't find out until later that he had a wife in another city."

"I'm sorry," Nora murmured, easily able to sympathize with the other woman's betrayal.

Mrs. Turner lifted her chin. "I'm afraid there was a scandal, although my father managed to hush up most of it. Still, there are always people who delight in other's mistakes. I'm sure you know the kind to whom I refer."

"Yes, I do," Nora replied instantly.

Mrs. Turner smiled, a warm, genuine expression that lit up her eyes. "They aren't worth our time."

"No."

"My story is long in the past. But your situation has reminded me so much of it." Mrs. Turner leaned forward, her tone suddenly decisive. "You can't allow yourself to be bullied any longer by Wilma Worthington and Shirley Burton, you know. They'll never leave you alone until you make them respect you."

"How?" Nora asked. "I thought if I went on with my life and stayed out of trouble—"

She stopped, realizing how that must sound. With Bret's help, she'd ended up escalating the scandal. "I thought things would die down," she finished painfully.

Mrs. Turner shook her head, leaned forward, and put a hand on Nora's where it rested in her lap. "What you must do now is stand up to them. Use your strong points to command their respect."

"My strong points?"

"Your riding." She straightened in her chair, a small triumphant smile playing on her lips. "I remember the pictures of you in the Wichita Falls paper when you won blue ribbons at your riding competitions."

"Just pony club events."

"Regardless. Your riding and your qualifications to teach are the only things that are anybody's business."

"That's right," Nora agreed, still stunned by support from such unexpected quarters.

"I don't care if you had affairs with all of Richie Worthington's bosses. It's your life to run."

"Well, yes," faltered Nora, "but I didn't—"

"Of course not. But whether you did or didn't isn't the most important thing," Sara Turner waved her protest aside. "I've thought about this and I think I have just the thing."

Nora looked at her in fascination. "You have?"

"Yes. You need to enter the Association Race next week."

"What?" That was the last thing Nora had expected to hear. Sure, she'd considered entering the race, just to give Bret a run for his money. He needed to be taken down several notches.

"Yes, my dear." The older woman's face was eager. "I'm quite serious. I think it would be very effective."

"Why?"

"Now don't tell me that you can't give those old cowboys some competition," Mrs. Turner chided.

"Of course I could," Nora acknowledged slowly.

"What better way to demonstrate your riding ability

to a bunch of horse people than winning their annual race?'' she demanded triumphantly.

''I—I'm not a member of the Association.''

''That's not a problem,'' Mrs. Turner replied promptly. ''I'll sponsor you.''

''That . . . that would be wonderful of you.''

''Nonsense.'' The older woman looked at her expectantly. ''Well, will you do it?''

''Bret's won for the last ten years,'' Nora blurted out.

Mrs. Turner was silent for a moment before she shrugged. ''Every race is a new race.''

Nora hesitated. The thought of beating him was irresistible. What if she could win both the race and the land? She'd steal his local legend status, his title and his damned landing strip in one sweep. He deserved to be beaten in more than just the race. How much more despicable could a man be than to make love to a woman while plotting to steal her dream?

Rage and hurt rose up in Nora. He had to be punished.

''You know, my dear,'' Mrs. Turner broke into her thoughts. ''You'll have to work out your private life yourself. I can't pretend any special knowledge in that arena. Bret Maddock's always been a handful.''

She rose from her seat. ''Still, he's not a bad boy. If you do decide to enter the race, he'll play fair.''

He doesn't play fair! Nora's bruised heart protested.

''You think it over, my dear,'' Sara Turner said, as she turned to go, ''and let me know.''

Nora stood up slowly, watching her unexpected benefactress leave. Why not race Chessie against Bret? Winning would insure that Bret would never want to bed her again, would most likely never even talk to her. And she could take on the whole town as well . . .

"I'll do it," Nora declared decisively. "And I'm very grateful for your help."

Mrs. Turner turned back, clasping Nora's hand in hers. "That's my girl. I knew you had the courage."

Chapter Ten

A tightening line of tension played along Nora's nerves. This was it, D-day. Soon, she'd walk into the crowd outside and challenge Bret for the championship.

In the week since their discovery in the mud, he'd called and come by the house countless times. Each time she'd refused to talk to him, knowing he'd only tell her more lies.

Still, he kept stopping by.

"Steady, girl." Nora ran the currycomb over Chessie's coat. The mare huffed a breath through her nostrils as if trying to assimilate the new smells of a strange stall. The barn was empty, the other racers having already left. Outside, the noise of the Association Chaparral Playday could be heard through the stable's open doors.

Maybe if she hadn't been fool enough to let him get close to her heart, she wouldn't be suffering now. How could she have let herself fall in love with such a snake?

So much depended on her winning the race today. She wanted to rub his face in the dirt, to hurt him as much as he'd hurt her. At this point, the scandal and the gossip mattered very little.

Nora smoothed Chessie one last time, reaching for the comb to straighten her mane. Bret had done her greater harm than Richard ever could. He'd lured her to laugh, had made her long for his love. Yet, all his admonitions to take chances had been offered for devious reasons. He'd even lied about loving her.

Nora pushed the thought away, unable to allow herself doubt at this point. She had to go forward, had to carve out a life for herself. Unsure of whether she would stay in Stoneburg or leave for a more hospitable place, all she knew now was that she had to beat Bret.

Intent on her methodical preparations for the race, she didn't hear her name until it was repeated directly behind her.

"Nora!"

She spun around and saw Richard in the open stall door.

"My God, Nora, what are you doing here?"

Surprised to see him, she responded without thinking, "Getting ready to race."

"Do you think that's a good idea?" He stepped forward, crowding Chessie, who danced sideways. "With all the talk?"

Nora grasped her halter. "Step back, Richard."

Speaking in a low tone, she gentled the mare. She had no idea why Richard was back in town. He'd never cared about the Association's activities any more than its annual barbecues.

Was he back today to create another scene in front of everyone? The memory of their last meeting was still fresh in her mind. After his behavior at the benefit, she was easily able to believe the worst of him. But she couldn't let Richard disturb her concentration now. It would take all her focus to win the race ahead.

"I'm really busy now, Richard," Nora said curtly, reaching for Chessie's bridle from the hook. Her mind turned back to the race. *Should she have walked the course again? Maybe a fourth time would have revealed some hidden quirk to the terrain.*

"I guess you're surprised to see me back in town so soon," Richard said, not taking her hint.

She glanced up briefly. "Ah . . . yes, I guess so." *Did Bret know yet that she was challenging him?* Slipping the bridle over Chessie's head, Nora forced her thoughts away from Bret.

"You know better than anyone that work keeps me pretty busy this time of year." Richard laughed self-importantly. "Well, it keeps me busy all the time."

"Yes, I know," she jumped in, cutting his monologue short. "Could we talk later, Richard? Chessie and I need to get ready."

He glanced at the horse. "She looks fine. Actually, I have something very important to say. Something you'll want to hear."

Quelling the bulk of her impatience, Nora turned to him. "Well, tell me then and let me get back to work."

"Okay," he said, looking momentarily disconcerted. "I've been fired."

"Oh." For the life of her, Nora couldn't think of anything to say. Cheering would have been too crass, but condolences were beyond her. She fell silent, still getting Chessie ready.

"It was completely unfair," he declared, apparently unaware of her lack of interest. "Benson acted on a trumped-up sexual harassment charge. They couldn't even be more original than that! It's a trendy issue."

He laughed sarcastically. "But I know the real reason. It had nothing to do with groping some secretary. I was doing too well, showing Benson up with the big management. So he just fired me!"

Nora would have bet that several secretaries were relieved to see Richard go. She felt a momentary flash of disgust at herself for not recognizing his true character years before. Had he always been such a self-absorbed bore? At least, Bret had the advantage of being charming.

"That's too bad," Nora said, trying to soothe Richard just enough to get rid of him. "Well, maybe we'll have time to talk about it later."

"But don't you understand?" He stood in the stall opening, his face impatient. "Don't you see what this means to us?"

"Us?" Nora repeated, thunderstruck. "What us?"

"I'm trying to tell you that I made a mistake when I broke it off." He stepped forward again, sending Chessie sidling away.

"Richard, you have to stay out of the stall." Nora moved to the doorway, pushing him in front of her. He apparently wasn't going away before he had his say.

He allowed her to urge him back into the walkway, taking the opportunity to catch her hand in his. "I want us to put all this behind us. Start fresh somewhere else. I'll find another job, maybe in a different state. And you can join me. It'll be just like old times." Richard smiled down at her fondly.

Nora stared at him, trying to understand how any individual could so completely create a false reality in his own mind. He needed her now, so she was supposed to wipe out the past four months as if they'd never happened?

"I know you're probably worried that I'll hold your fling with Bret Maddock against you, but I'm sure I'll be able to get over it," he said magnanimously.

Nora jerked her hand away. "You don't need to take the trouble, because I'm not interested."

"Now, Nora," he chided. "Don't fib. The whole town knows you've been rolling in the dirt with that cowboy."

"Rolling in the mud," she corrected furiously. "And I mean that I'm not interested in *you!*"

"Nora. Sweetheart." Richard tried to take her hand again but she evaded him. "You don't mean that. I know you're hurt. I shouldn't have reacted the way I did about that incident with Benson. But I was crazed with jealousy. To think the woman I loved and my boss . . . well, you'd both been drinking. . . ."

"I had not been drinking," Nora nearly shouted. "And you knew I didn't do anything to make him paw me like that. You knew! But I'd inadvertently become a liability to your career, so you dumped me!"

"No!"

"Yes," she said scathingly, "and now that you've fallen off the fast track, you think I'll let you back in my life. Well, you're wrong. I just want you to go away."

"Nora, you can't be serious. I need you," he declared, suddenly tearful.

She stared at him, the peculiar irony of the situation almost making her smile. If Richard weren't so adept at manipulating people, she might have believed his emotion.

"Well, I don't need you." Nora turned on her heel.

She hoisted the riding saddle from its stand, shutting out Richard's sputtering half-sentences.

She couldn't let him distract her anymore. The race had to be the only thing in her mind. She felt as if she were on the verge of the biggest moment in her life. In the next half hour, she'd prove her riding ability and get her revenge against Bret.

"Nora!" Richard implored from the walkway outside the stall.

"Go away." Her hands went through each task methodically.

"You're distracted," Richard said reluctantly. "We'll talk later."

"Whatever." She didn't look up as he left, making a mental note to be very busy in the next few days. He might be convinced there was more to talk about, but she had nothing more to say.

Tightening the last strap, Nora straightened as Richard's retreating steps echoed in the stables. She drew in a deep breath, feeling clean and resolved. She might still have a splintered heart over Bret, but at least Richard was well and truly out of her life.

Taking Chessie's reins in hand, she led the mare out of the stall and through the walkway to the outdoors. Each step took them closer to the moment of truth. This was her opportunity to show the people of Stoneburg that she could ride with the best and face down the cheap scandalmongers.

She picked up her riding helmet and fastened the strap under her chin.

Come hell or high water, she was determined to win. If Stoneburg wanted to attribute a scarlet past to her, let them. She was here to teach riding, dammit. And for that, she was well equipped.

I love you, Bret's words echoed in her head. Nora tried to ignore the tightening in her stomach.

All her life she'd known that love was bought at a price. One she couldn't pay.

Nora stepped out into the sunshine, registering its warmth through her white cotton shirt. She'd dressed to please herself today, snug jeans tucked into riding boots. She might not look like Annie Oakley, but she was determined to beat the pants off every man in the race.

Winning would insure that Bret would never again smile at her with that crooked, charming grin. He'd never chase her, never try to pull her close and kiss her silly. In taking his title, she knew she'd be shaming him in front of the whole county. He'd never want to bed her again.

As she walked toward the starting line, she tried to be eager for that moment.

Outside the barn, the whole town seemed to be clustered around the starting post. Nora walked Chessie forward, knowing that most of these people weren't aware of her late entry into the race. She ignored the curious looks and turned toward the starting line.

Keeping her steps steady, she moved through the crowd, meeting the stares without expression. Walking the race course three times in the last few days had burned it into her memory.

She knew every small stone, every hillock that might make Chessie stumble.

The course spread out over the Smith's back pasture, a straight line starting outside the barn and heading down to a tall, beribboned pole erected at the end of the pasture. The riders had to grab a ribbon as they rounded the pole. The first rider to return to the start line, ribbon in hand, won the race.

Slowly, Nora walked through the crowd, making her way to the starting line. Noise seemed to ripple around her, hissing, half-quiet comments. She felt the conjecture, sensed the surprise and brushed aside the accompanying flutter of anxiety it brought to her stomach.

A makeshift platform, bales of hay stacked together, had been created next to the start line. An older man she didn't recognize stood on the platform, holding a microphone.

Beyond the platform, several mounted riders were lined up waiting for the start.

Nora's heart thundered as she caught a glimpse of Bret, his dark hair covered by a cowboy hat.

"I have an announcement to make," the man with the microphone called out. "We have a late entry in this race—Miss Nora Hampton, riding her mare, Chessie."

A muffled chuckle followed his words as a surprised murmur ran through the crowd.

Bret swiveled in her direction, astonishment on his face.

Nora moved forward, clamping her teeth together with determination. Stopping Chessie beside the hay platform, she swung up into the saddle.

There were ten racers in all, drawn more by the prestige of winning than by the modest cash prize. Nora urged Chessie forward, talking softly to the mare as she brought her into line.

She could feel Bret's eyes on her, but she refused to look his way.

Patting Chessie, Nora took a deep breath to steady herself as the announcer began to describe the race.

"You didn't tell me you were going to race." Bret leaned over to say in a low voice, as the man with the microphone talked.

"No, I didn't." She couldn't meet his eyes and

keep her equilibrium, so Nora stared over Chessie's ears.

"Hey, Bret!" A male voice from the crowd called out. "How about the loser has to do the winner a personal favor?"

The nearest bystanders laughed, the innuendo obvious with the gossip running rampant about them. Nora clenched her jaw.

"Bret wouldn't want nothin' from those cowboys," another man yelled amid the hooting laughter drawn by the first remark.

"Let's get this race started," the announcer cut into the raucousness. "Racers, on your mark. Get ready."

Next to her, Bret and the other riders seemed to tense.

Nora balanced the reins in her hands, every muscle taut as she crouched in the saddle. "Let's show them, Chessie," she murmured low. "Let's make them eat dirt and die."

Crack! The starting pistol sounded.

With a bound, they left the starting line. Nora leaned forward, balancing her weight over Chessie's forelegs. They flew over the ground, the thunder of the horse's hooves around them.

From the first, Bret was out in front. Nora felt Chessie straining forward, the spirit of competition driving the mare to overtake Bret's stallion and leave the other horses behind.

Nora held Chessie back, reining her in with the slightest pressure. They had to hold steady now, keeping just back of Bret until the first fourth of the course was behind them. Chessie was the swiftest horse Nora had ever ridden, but they needed to make their move at just the right moment.

Bret rode ahead of her, his powerful back tensed

and forward, every fiber of him thrown into winning. The shock in his face had said it all. Never had it occurred to him that she might be a serious challenge.

The thought spurred Nora on and she loosened the reins, letting Chessie take the bit more firmly. The mare gradually gained on General, her strong stride eating up the distance.

The beribboned pole stood ahead. Nora measured the yards, knowing they had to gain on Bret now or lose the race.

Tightening her heels against Chessie's flanks, she gave the mare her head.

The ground seemed to fall away, wind whistling past them as Chessie came up beside General and gradually pulled ahead. Nora saw Bret's sideways glance and registered the surprise on his face. He had to have known she was on his tail, but Chessie's speed probably came as a shock.

They galloped over the pasture, side by side, the two cowboys lengths behind them. Nora struggled to block out Bret's presence. She leaned forward further, calling out to Chessie. They had to give it their all.

Picking up speed, the mare lengthened the distance between them and Bret. She flew along over the turf, guided by Nora's steady hands, avoiding the soft spots, the uneven patches of ground.

With Bret at their heels, they had to secure their lead. Nora couldn't be sure of beating him around the pole in close quarters and she didn't want to be there at the same time he was.

As they approached the pole, she reined Chessie back just enough to make the turn.

With the reins held tight in her left hand, she grabbed at a ribbon.

The sliver of fabric slipped through her fingers.

All too aware of the approaching riders, Bret out in front, she bit back a sob and wildly grabbed again.

Just as she grasped the ribbon, Bret's horse thundered toward her.

Her prize clenched in her fist, Nora set Chessie flying toward the finish line, flattening herself over the horse's neck.

The home stretch lay before them. Nora could hear the thunder of hooves behind and knew Bret was on her heels. She poured everything into the moment, using every ounce of horsemanship she possessed to communicate with Chessie.

They raced back over the pasture, the horses running full out. General hung at Chessie's tail as they tore toward the barns. Nora could feel the excitement of the horse beneath her, feel the mare's thrill for the race.

The cheers of the crowd seemed to rise up to greet them as they pelted closer and closer. Nora heard the din, a clamoring racket in her ears muffled by the reverberation of her own heartbeat.

Closer and closer they came, Bret gaining on her, inch by inch.

Everything seemed in slow motion. The finish line lay straight ahead. Nora's ears were filled with the pounding thunder of the horse's hooves, the frenzied cheering of the crowd and the throb of adrenaline through her body.

Her eyes glued on the finish, she urged Chessie forward, her breath clutched in her throat as they raced toward the finish.

It was over in an instant. Chessie and Nora raced across the line, just a half length in front of Bret.

Dazed and overwhelmed that she'd actually won, Nora reined Chessie in and found herself off the mare, surrounded by a cheering crowd that urged her toward the makeshift platform.

A cowboy took Chessie from her, yelling, "I'll cool her off," as excited onlookers pulled Nora toward the announcer.

Some part of her brain registered that the other riders had crossed the line. Her quick look around failed to locate Bret, however. Had he simply ridden off?

"My God, girl! Where'd you learn to ride like that?" A grizzled cowboy clapped her on the back as she was swept forward.

Eager hands helped her up on the mounded bales of hay.

"Hey, Bret!" a voice called. "A woman brought you down."

"Ain't that the truth," Bret responded, his voice drawing Nora's gaze.

He stood off to the far right, hat off, his eyes meeting hers when she finally spotted him.

Nora felt the jolt of impact and saw something in his face that she couldn't identify. There was no resentment at her win, just a burning impression of intensity in his eyes.

Shaken, Nora looked away, still dazed by the turn of events. The crowd was talking excitedly.

"I never thought I'd see ol' Bret beat so bad." Several ranch hands standing nearby snickered loudly. "How the mighty have fallen."

Behind the group of cowboys, Nora saw Richard's mother standing next to Sara Burton. Cissy was nowhere in sight, but the expression on the older women's faces said it all. If she'd won some hearts today, theirs weren't among them.

Nora couldn't have cared less.

She smiled at the two women, enjoying their surprise in response to her gesture.

Suddenly, their enmity didn't matter. She was through worrying about other people's opinions.

"All right, folks," the announcer called out. "Quiet now. We have a trophy to give out here. Miz Hampton," he spoke into the microphone, "it's my great honor to present you with the Association's trophy for the best rider in Montague County."

Nora clasped the statue of horse and rider in trembling hands.

"This is the first time in ten years," the announcer went on, "that this award hasn't gone to Bret Maddock—"

A cheer rose from the crowd.

"—and the first time, ever, that it's gone to a woman."

More applause greeted this.

"And may I say," the man took Nora's hand, "what a pleasure it is to have such a beautiful woman up here instead of some old weather-beaten cowboy."

As the crowd laughed, the announcer handed Nora the microphone.

For a long moment, she could do no more than clutch it. A welter of emotions held her voice captive—relief, excitement and satisfaction among them.

In the back of the crowd, she spotted Mrs. Turner.

Nora cleared her throat. "Thank you," she said, meeting the older woman's gaze over the heads of those clustered around her. "I want to thank everyone here, especially Mrs. Turner, for her encouragement and sponsorship."

Energetic applause rose in response to her words.

Glancing down as she handed back the microphone, Nora was surprised to see Bret standing in front of her.

Without a word, he reached out and scooped her into his arms

"What are you doing?" she gasped as the crowd around them began laughing and calling out.

"We've got to work out that personal favor from the loser to the winner." Bret pitched his reply so those near could hear as he strode through the bystanders.

Knowing her embarrassment was all too visible, Nora hissed, "Put me down!"

"Just hang on to that trophy," Bret recommended. "It may not be mine this year, but I still wouldn't want you to drop it."

Not wanting to look any sillier than she already did, Nora decided not to try struggling out of his grasp. Instead, she followed his recommendation and clutched the statue more tightly.

Unfortunately, being carried in his arms felt like the most natural thing in the world.

When he finally deposited her on her feet, they stood beside his pickup truck. He opened the passenger door for her.

Nora stood there, eyeing him without getting in.

"I'm a very determined man," Bret said softly. "You wouldn't talk to me before, so we're going to talk now."

She looked at him, knowing her own stubbornness had to be reflected in her face.

"Please?" he asked with that crooked smile. "You wouldn't make a man pour out his heart in public, would you?"

Nora got into the truck. If they had to have this conversation, she didn't want an audience, either.

Besides, she loved him, and her heart demanded that she at least listen to his story, even if he were lying through his teeth.

"What about Chessie?" she asked, once he'd gotten in and started the engine.

"The hands will take her back to the ranch," he assured her.

Nora fell silent as they drove, unsure and confused by the turn of events. Did he really expect to be able to lie his way out of this?

And yet, every crazy instinct urged her to give him the benefit of the doubt. Was he really devious enough to set her up for scandal? How could she love him this much if he were so evil?

Her thoughts in a whirl, she didn't realize he'd driven to the Turner property until they arrived there. She glanced at him sideways as they turned into the disused, overgrown driveway.

When he stopped the pickup in front of the house and got out without comment, she didn't know what to do but follow him.

Bret crossed the front yard and climbed the steps that had been the scene of their heated passion on that afternoon so many weeks before.

Opening the front door without hesitation, Bret held it wide for her.

"It was locked before," she said.

"I got the key from Mrs. Turner." His face was serious. "I wanted to talk to you here. Go in."

She stepped over the threshold and found herself in a spacious front room with large sash windows and a cozy fireplace. At one end of the room was a wall of built-in bookcases, and to the side of the fireplace sat an ancient wooden rocker.

"Why are we here?" Her voice trembled with the weight of might-have-beens. More than the house, she mourned the loss of him—his laughter and the warmth of being in his arms.

Bret had said he loved her, and the words haunted her still. She'd wanted his love so much.

"This place started all the trouble between us," he said. "It seemed like the best place to tell you how wrong I've been."

"What?" She turned to study his face.

He stood facing her in the empty room, his back to the sunlit windows. "I screwed up this thing between us pretty bad."

Nora didn't know what to say.

Shoving his hands into his pockets, Bret took a step toward the fireplace and turned back to face her. "I've always wanted you, Nora. Probably since we were teenagers. But until this week, I didn't realize how much you've come to mean to me."

Nora's heart stopped beating.

He ran a hand through his hair, the gesture loaded with an awkward frustration she'd never seen in him before. "Dammit, I'm so used to finessing things, so used to finding ways to make everything come out . . . that I got careless with you."

Her mind grappled with the implications of his words.

"I'm a risk-taker, Nora. It's what I do. I run close to the line in everything I do. Hell, just ask my mother. I ran her ragged as a kid." He turned to pace back toward the window. "And basically, pushing the limits has worked out pretty well for me."

Bret faced her again. "I meant what I said that day we got stuck in the mud. I love you. I never meant to hurt you, and I swear, I never planned any of this stuff to keep you from getting this land. The Burtons showed up out of nowhere, I swear."

Why she should believe him was beyond her, but she felt herself weakening. That he stood here at all, saying these things after she'd publicly beaten him, was even more astonishing.

"When you first came back to town, I wanted to help you with the gossipy old broads." He stopped and looked her straight in the face. "I also wanted to sleep with you. Really, really wanted to make love with you."

Nora looked at him, unsure of what his confession meant. "I think the old broads will hate me till I die."

A smile broke over his face then. "Boy, you showed them today. I could have cheered."

"You *wanted* to lose the race?" she gasped.

"Hell, no." Bret grinned. "I did my best to beat you. And I'll bet you money that next year, I'll have another horse to give you and Chessie a run for your money. But when you crossed that finish line like a demon on that mare, anyone who appreciates great horsemanship had to cheer."

"You didn't mind my beating you?" Nora asked incredulously.

He crossed the room to where she stood. "What I mind is you thinking that I'd cheat you out of something. That I'd make love to you while I'm plotting behind your back. I didn't betray you, Nora, not really. I just didn't tell you all the truth."

She swallowed hard against the lump in her throat.

Bret went on, his gaze intent on her face, "I didn't tell you about my bid on this land because I knew how you felt about it and I didn't want to lose my chance with you. I wasn't sure you'd actually get to the point of trying to buy the land. So I didn't say anything to you about it."

Shoving his hands in his back pockets, he took another agitated turn in front of the windows. "I wasn't completely honest with you and I'm sorry."

Nora looked up into his face, beginning to tremble.

"I called Mrs. Turner three days ago," Bret said, "and withdrew my offer on the land. I think she'd already made up her mind to sell it to you, but I'm not buying the property one way or the other."

"What?"

"It's yours," he said softly. "Build your dream here, only let me be a part of it. Don't kick me out of your life."

Tears blurred Nora's vision, a sob of relief tight in her chest.

Taking an unconscious step forward, she found herself in his arms, the strength of his embrace holding her steady against his thudding heart.

"I love you, Nora," he whispered unsteadily against her temple. "I want to live with you forever."

His kiss seared her and she felt the trembling of his body against hers. As impossible as it seemed, he was offering her everything—all her hopes, all her dreams.

Bret straightened, his eyes locked with hers. "I'm asking you to take the biggest risk. Will you marry me? I can't say I won't give you grief sometimes, but I promise to love you faithfully, always."

"That's all I could ever want," Nora whispered shakily as he drew her nearer.

Moments later, their breathing ragged and heavy, Bret whispered, "If you let me put in my landing strip, I might even help you pay the note."

Laughing as she buried her face against his shoulder, Nora knew she was signing on for the ride of her life.

ABOUT THE AUTHOR

Carol Rose lives in Texas with her softball-playing husband of twenty years and her two rambunctious teenage daughters. A longtime romance reader herself, she enjoys writing realistic stories about people who could be her neighbors. Carol's always interested in hearing readers' likes and dislikes and can be contacted at: P.O. Box 8171, Fort Worth, TX 76124.